Jump Rope Queen
AND OTHER STORIES

Karen Loeb

LOEB

Minnesota Voices Project Winner

NEW RIVERS PRESS 1992

Copyright © 1993 by Karen Loeb
Library of Congress Catalog Card Number 92-64073
ISBN 0-89823-145-0
All Rights Reserved
Edited by Susan Welch
Editorial Assistance by Paul J. Hintz
Cover Painting by Karen Tucker Kuykendall
Book Design and Typesetting by Peregrine Publications

The publication of *Jump Rope Queen* has been made possible by generous grants from the Jerome Foundation and the Metropolitan Regional Arts Council (from an appropriation by the Minnesota Legislature). Additional support has been provided by the First Bank System Foundation, Liberty State Bank, the National Endowment for the Arts (with funds appropriated by the Congress of the United States), the Star Tribune/Cowles Media Company, the Tennant Company Foundation, the United Arts Fund, and the contributing members of New Rivers Press. New Rivers Press also wishes to acknowledge the Minnesota Non-Profits Assistance Fund for its invaluable support.

All characters in these stories are fictitious; any resemblance between them and real people, living or dead, is coincidental.

New Rivers Press books are distributed by:

The Talman Company
131 Spring Street, Suite 201 E-N
New York NY 10012

Bookslinger
2402 University Avenue West
Saint Paul MN 55114

Jump Rope Queen has been manufactured in the United States of America for New Rivers Press, 420 N. 5th Street/Suite 910, Minneapolis, MN 55401 in a first edition of 2,000 copies.

Acknowledgements

Some of the stories were published in the following places:

"The World Traveler" in *Korone 5*; reprinted in *Upriver 4*

"Family Meetings" in *The Chattahoochee Review*

"The Koquettes" in *The Wooster Review*

"The Sadie Hawkins Day Dance" in *Bloodroot*

"Going Under" in *The Village Advocate* and *The Orlando Sentinel*. A PEN Syndicated Fiction Award Winner.

"Henry Africa's" in *The North American Review*; reprinted in *The Story Workshop Reader* and *Itinerary 4*

"Uncertain Geographies" in *Korone 6*

"Madame Alexander" in *Lullwater Review*

"The Bachelors" in *Habersham Review*

The author is very grateful to the Virginia Center for the Creative Arts for giving her time to write some of the stories in this collection. She also thanks the Wisconsin Arts Board for its fellowship and grant that allowed her to keep summers free to write.

To David Dial

Contents

Chicago

Jump Rope Queen

JUMP ROPE QUEEN of the neighborhood dashes in and out of ropes like a cat   challenges everyone   I can jump longer, I can jump faster, I can stay in past anyone, I can double-dutch. Jump rope queen is 8 years old   wears a leather jacket   used to belong to her uncle   flew a bomber   it has a fur collar and zippered pockets. We yell, hey jump rope queen, your jacket's too big but secretly we want it. Jump rope queen is a roving menace   she breaks into everyone's game all along the schoolyard fence

> Fudge fudge call the judge
> Mama's gonna have a baby
> Wrap it in tissue paper
> Throw it down the elevator
> First floor – MISS!
> Second floor – MISS!
> Third floor – MISS!
> Fourth floor – KICK IT OUT THE DOOR!

They say she doesn't have parents but I don't believe it. They say she lives with her teenage brother in an apartment hotel and they cook dinner themselves   mostly eat bologna sandwiches on white bread

Jump rope queen sometimes gets a ride to school on her brother Manny's motorcycle   little wooden box attached to the cycle   she climbs out   I looked once   there's a bench inside with a red cushion

Jump rope queen is never a turner only a jumper
51 52 53 54

She can jump higher   she can jump more. Jump rope queen wears gym shoes with high tops like boys   black with white soles and laces   Keds printed on the heels   doesn't wear a petticoat   when she jumps her skirt inflates up   does full splits when the song is chanted   gravel etching her legs

> Postman, postman do your duty
> Here comes Alma, the American Beauty
> She can do the splits
> She can wear her dresses
> Way up to her hips.

Jump rope queen catches us in the bathroom looking in the mirror   piece of metal made shiny   she's in her black high top shoes and bomber jacket   says we are sissies because our dresses stick out and crunch if you bump against them

We like them that way we like them that way, we taunt. The stick-out wears out and we dip them in starch. My stick-out slip was hanging over head and dripped on me while I was in the tub, Jeannie says – my hair got all stiff

Jump rope queen sniffs. Her hair is ratty never combed   no one brushes it for her or puts barrettes in or braids it   no one washes it and combs it out wet for her. Jump rope queen has hair that zigzags on the bottom   get dizzy looking at it. Jump rope queen always looks as if she's crying   eyes red puffy

> Little Sally Saucer
> Crying in the water
> Cry Sally cry
> Wipe off your eyes

We dance around her singing in the room marked GIRLS. She gets a mean look on her face   pushes through the circle   pops open the door   flies out. Wish I could run so fast. Her shoes squeak on the hallway floor. Those shoes are what let her run like that   Jump rope queen always wears those shoes even in winter in the snow, even on picture day when everyone gets dressed up   shiny shoes with buckles   jump rope queen wears her high top gym shoes and doesn't smile

My shoes are brown oxfords with air holes so the feet can breathe. There's a machine in the store that turns my feet green and lets me see my toes through the leather. Mr. Howell looks in one viewer   says wiggle and I can see my toes squirm in the green fog of the x-ray. He sells shoes to all the children in the neighborhood   gives a balloon that says HOWELL'S KIDDY KICKS SHOES   jump rope queen never has a balloon   she wears gym shoes all the time and my mother says she'll ruin her feet

How wonderful to ruin your feet. My best friend Cynthia ruins her feet every day in her black patent shoes she wears with white angora socks. My black patents are safely in the closet smothered in Vaseline   waiting for the perfect moment   special occasion visit, for Sunday school, for a coronation

Cynthia lives in a hotel   12 flights up   barbershop in the lobby   we walk up sometimes just to feel our hearts pump fast. We place our hands on each other's heart and feel the vibration. Cynthia's hair is golden brown and pulled back into a tight pony tail   she wears felt skirts with poodles appliqued on them and angora socks. She dresses as I imagine an angel does. In the schoolyard she jumps carefully so she doesn't mess her clothes   holds her feet close together

> Ice cream soda, ginger ale, pop
> Tell me the name of my sweetheart
> A, B, C, D, E, F, Geee....

Jump rope queen dashes into the rope   end slides out of my hand with a burn   Cynthia falls   scrapes her leg   blood all over her felt skirt   Oh, Rachel, MRS. PEARLS WILL KILL ME, she sobs

Who's Mrs. Pearls? I ask

You know, she says – our maid – SHE'LL KILL ME. We all look at jump rope queen who stands by the flagpole and doesn't say anything. Our eyes tell her to get lost

Cynthia's hotel room is a vast apartment with rugs so thick I bounce with each step   different color phone in each room. There is a red phone in the living room. The phone in my house is black and heavy, metal dial with the paint worn off. We go to

Cynthia's after school   not often   can't make noise and it's hard to play without noise. One day I find out why we have to be quiet. We're sitting on the floor walking our paper dolls around – suddenly a voice calls out

Cyn-thi-a.

Cynthia bolts up, smooths down her skirt says c'mon. I follow her down the hall. The bedroom is golden, full of curlicues. We've discovered where King Midas put his treasure. The bed is twice as big as my parents' bed, jumbled with covers that shine, and they are moving. From out of the wrinkles comes a lady's head, blonde hair feathery hand with sparkling rings fumbles for a glass with brown liquid. Whiskey. I know because my father represents a liquor company and he brings a lot of it home   I can smell it across the room

Who's that? I ask

My mother, Cynthia whispers. Isn't she pretty?

Who's your friend? her mother asks

Rachel, Cynthia says

Well, make sure she doesn't wear any of your clothes. We spend a fortune on your clothes and we don't want them getting messed up. I'm sure . . . *Rachel* understands.

I tug on my plaid cotton dress and stand crooked on my brown oxford   wish I were anywhere but in front of this woman with the drowsy voice. Next time I go there my mother weaves ribbons into my braids and I wear my own felt skirt with a poodle – somehow my mother saved and bought me one. Mrs. Pearls the large bosomed maid in the black and white uniform, accuses me of stealing one of Cynthia's skirts. But still I envy Cynthia. Hotel life is exotic. Elevator to your house. Sometimes we ride up and down up and down till we get yelled at

Jump rope queen lives in a hotel too. Nobody visits her but we see her go in after school   Picadilly Hotel where the White Sox stay when they're in town. My brother stands outside and waits for autographs and invites the players home for dinner. Nellie Fox   Sherman Lollar   Luis Aparicio. They never come

Cynthia and I form a club   call a meeting at my house across the street from Cynthia's hotel. Jeannie Winters who always has a cold sore, and the twins Arlene and Eileen who I can tell apart by the different color saddles on their saddle shoes, and all the girls in our group, the ones who wear crinkly petticoats, pile through the door

The twins have asked none other than Alma Louise Witherspoon, jump rope queen. She wears the black and white gym shoes no bomber jacket. She has on about five sweaters instead. Legs red from the fall breeze. Someone has made long sausage curls in her hair, called rag curls because you wind torn-apart cloth in your hair. She looks proud sitting on the sagging leather couch between the twins, tapping her foot in the air. Why you wearing sweaters, Alma Louise? Jeannie asks. Where's your coat? Jump rope queen squints at her but doesn't answer. Cynthia is sitting with her hands in a tight ball not looking at jump rope queen. She's still burned from when she got knocked down

Twins are crazy for bringing her but we go on with the meeting. I show my red cardboard heart box from last Valentine's Day, slot gashed in it. We talk about making wreaths out of hangers and crepe paper for Christmas, and pass around the heart for the dues. Everyone puts money in except jump rope queen. Arlene in the blue saddles says, I've got extra, I'll put in for her

NO, Cynthia says. Everyone pays alone. Then she says we should name the club. I want to call it the After School Club for Girls

HEY, Cynthia says. Let's call it the 9½ club.

It sounds okay, but we all want to know why. Cynthia looks at us amazed. Why? Because Alma Louise is only half a person.

It gets so quiet I can hear my pink cat clock ticking in the hallway upstairs, its tail going back and forth. Jeannie picks at the cold sore that is sprawled on the side of her mouth each of the twins takes one of jump rope queen's hands. That was a dumb thing to say, Eileen in the brown saddles says. No one answers, no one agrees or disagrees. Suddenly there are little hiccups coming from jump rope queen curls bobbing up and down rush to the door open it the twins follow and three other girls. Doesn't anyone want to make a wreath? I wail, but now it's only Cynthia and me left

*

They announce a jump rope contest in school   whoever wins
gets to go to another school to compete until there's the best
jump roper in the city. No one from the club meeting is speak-
ing. We all bring our own ropes to school and jump alone. Cyn-
thia isn't talking to me because I'm mad at her for ruining our
club. The twins aren't talking to Cynthia because of what she
said to jump rope queen and they aren't talking to me because
I had the club meeting. For the past two weeks jump rope queen
has brought her own rope, making her feet spit gravel as she
does crossies and kicks. We turn our ropes and pretend not to
see but every once in a while we're caught watching her cross
her arms and uncross the rope in back of her. I can do that,
Jeannie says, but she ends up with the rope snarled around her
ankles

Cynthia announces a truce. Alma Louise has to be in our group
if we're gonna win the contest, she says. No way we can beat
the big girls.

No one disagrees but jump rope queen is absent from school.
You coming with me, Rachel? Cynthia asks in the afternoon

Where you going?

To find HER. She bites her lip and looks to the sky

We walk across Hyde Park Boulevard   arms entwined because
there's a huge wind   snaps our dresses on our legs   bent over
we hope it won't pick us up and take us to Oz

The Picadilly hotel has a thick glass door that we have to push
open ourselves. At least we have a doorman in my hotel, Cyn-
thia says. We walk through the dark musty lobby arm in arm   I'm
ready to turn back but Cynthia goes right up to the desk and
I realize she knows what to do in hotels

WE'RE LOOKING FOR ALMA LOUISE WITHERSPOON,
she says in a loud voice to a white haired man in an undershirt

Fourth floor – 418, don't get your hand caught.

The elevator has an accordion grate   slides with a creak we
almost do get our hands caught. Inside Cynthia takes charge.
She presses the number 4.   A long time later we slide the grate

back. The hall has cooking odors in it. We finally see 418 and knock on the door

Man's voice asks, Who's there?

Let's go, I say. I tug on Cynthia's coat sleeve

Is Alma Louise Witherspoon there? Cynthia calls

Lock turns door opens. Manny, her brother steps back and we walk in. The room is bright full of boxes stacked up neatly. Jump rope queen is sitting at a table with metal legs, eating a bowl of soup stops, spoon in mid-air stares at us

Visitors for you, Manny says

You sick? Cynthia asks

Jump rope queen shakes her head

We have to talk to you. You tell her, Rachel.

So I tell her about the jump rope contest and won't she please be in it it'll mean we'll win and we're sorry about what happened at the club meeting. I'm mad that I have to apologize for Cynthia when she was the one who said Alma Louise was half a person

Jump rope queen licks a drop of soup from her spoon and glances at Manny who's putting clothes in a box

We're moving, she tells us

Cynthia frowns. When? But you can't. Not until the contest.

Jump rope queen looks at her brother again. We're moving tonight.

But why? I ask. Why can't it be after the contest?

The Thor-tees have found out about us, she says

What Thor-tees? Cynthia asks. We give each other a look

The Thor-tees. You know. The people who say you have to live with a mother or father.

Manny comes over to us. He has a crew-cut like my brother even though he's older. We heard someone turned us in. We're moving to another school district across town.

I've been to ten different schools, jump rope queen says. They haven't caught us yet. We don't have a mother or father. She said it like you'd say there was no more toast

So you can't jump for us? Cynthia asks, hoping she has heard wrong

We're moving later today, she says
The three of us are silent   looking at our shoes
Bye, I say. You're the best jumper I ever saw.
Jump rope queen smiles at me. It's the first time I ever saw her smile

Outside in the wind we lock arms again. Drat, Cynthia says. Now what are we going to do?

I don't want to tell her that probably jump rope queen will be competing against us. That if we make it to another level, Alma Louise might be there waiting to jump right over us

The wind makes dust in my eyes and I close them, letting Cynthia lead us along. Jump rope queen beat out a rhythm on the gravel in the school yard. She could act out the commands in Teddy Bear better than anyone

> Teddy Bear, Teddy Bear, turn around,
> Teddy Bear, Teddy Bear, touch the ground.
> Teddy Bear, Teddy Bear, show your shoes
> Teddy Bear, Teddy Bear, read the news.
> Teddy Bear, Teddy Bear, go upstairs,
> Teddy Bear, Teddy Bear, say your prayers
> Teddy Bear, Teddy Bear, blow out the light,
> Teddy Bear, Teddy Bear, say goodnight.

> GOODNIGHT!

Madame Alexander

DO YOU HAVE a doll that winds up
                    walks on tables   floors   rugs
                    talks a blue streak?
                            I do.
Do you have a doll that you can put real make-up on?
A doll with platinum hair that really grows?
A doll with golden hair and silver net stockings?
A doll as big as a baby that wears baby clothes?
                            I do.
Do you have a doll with a gray button on its tummy
    one on its back that you can press to shake its head
    yes or no?
                            I do.
A doll that cries and wets that you can feed with a
bottle?
A rag doll with red curls and button eyes that you have to
call Raggedy Ann because that's the name she comes
with?
                            I do.
Do you have a set of dolls small as pot holders   fit on one skinny
shelf   called Storybook dolls   long skirts
have names like
Scarlet

Amy
Jo
Hiawatha?

I do.

At night I line up dolls on my bed   put them around me   shape of a horseshoe   say goodnight to all of them. I never hold one   my teddy bear would be insulted. They sit there all night   dressed   ready for the next day.

Shadow of the dollhouse spreads over us in the moonbeams coming in through the window

The dollhouse family is asleep
I put them to bed
tiny people no bigger than my fingers
the father in the big bedroom
the brother in the green bedroom
the sister in the white bedroom with pink curtains
the mother in the guest room

*

Cynthia is over at my house playing dolls. Even she doesn't have as many as I do   even she fingers their dresses   hugs them to her   says that I have the best dolls of anybody. Her golden hair matches my Alice doll   my doll looks so perfect in her arms   like it really is her baby

Cynthia in her angora socks and angora collar that
ties in a bow
Alice in her blue dress and white pinafore
They are both ready to step through the looking glass.

Put her down, I say.

Cynthia sighs   looks around   hands me the Alice doll and takes up the sleeping doll   my no-name doll with the eyes that close with a click   big as a real baby

*

First saw the Alice doll in the window of Marshall Field's   dozens of dolls   pressed myself against the glass   squashed my face   I was already having dreams about them and I was wide awake

There were Alice dolls as big as a real girl down to Alice dolls no bigger than a hand   all dressed the same: blue dresses with white pinafores and golden hair   rabbit with a pocket watch and a mad hatter in the window but I didn't pay any attention   I stared at the Alice doll big as me and wanted it   I'd have a sister and she'd take me through the looking glass to have adventures.

Madame Alexander   magic words   Madame Alexander   they were on a white card in the corner of the huge window display and my mother read them to me: Alice in Wonderland by Madame Alexander. Didn't know who Madame Alexander was   never met her but she made dolls that cost a fortune   never had one   but this time my mother said she was going to put her foot down.

What does that mean? I asked.

She took my hand and pulled me from the window   you could almost hear a popping sound as I came unstuck from the glass.

Just you wait, my mother said.

Can we go into Field's? I asked. You know, to the fifth floor?

Some other time, my mother said.

We walked down State Street   glad to hold her hand   crowd of huge people   straw seats on the IC train home   Madame Alexander   Madame Alexander   Madame Alexander   Just you-wait   justyouwait   Madame Alexander   justyouwait

One afternoon   school day even   my mother said, Rachel, close your eyes, and I did,   said hold out your arms and I did   feel hear the soft crush of tissue paper   The moment of opening   like looking inside a flower   golden dust   instead it was the golden hair   the pink mouth   the blue dress   my mother and I stared at her for a long time

Let me hold her, my mother said.

I handed Alice to her, still in her blue tissue-paper cocoon. My mother cradled her   leaned over her   letting her long black hair streaked with silver fall in front, covering Alice for a moment.

Mama, your hair!

We both laughed and my mother scooped her hair back. She wore it down mostly   I brushed it weekend mornings.

She gave me back the doll   poking at my brown hair   pulling

at a barrette   didn't mind   had my doll   the best doll
ever Madame Alexander Madame Alexander
  Now Rachel, don't tell your father, my mother said.
  I looked up at her.
  At least not yet. It's our secret.

*

This time Cynthia says we're going to play at her house. Can't
argue we always play at my house so she gets a turn once in
a while. I don't even have to ask permission go there from school
just so I call home and tell my mother it's okay.
  Too much heat in Cynthia's apartment maid takes our
coats brushes off Cynthia's coat with a miniature broom the
shape of a small whiskey bottle doesn't brush mine Mrs. Pearls
is tall with gray-white skin the color of school paste wears a
black dress with white apron red hair in a bun like my mother
wears it when she goes out tells Cynthia and me to take off
our shoes so we don't mess the white carpet doesn't smile.
  Gotta call my mother, I say.
  Red phone in the living room. Yellow phone in the dining room.
White phone in the kitchen. Gold phone in the bathroom.
  Which one? Cynthia asks.
  Gold, I say.
  After I telephone we go to Cynthia's room to play. Mrs. Pearls
brings in milk and cookies. I grab a cookie Cynthia drinks her
milk eyes bobbing up at Mrs. Pearls   drinks the whole
glass and gasps for breath. Mrs. Pearls takes the glass her
feet squeak down on the thick carpet if it was grass blades
they'd be dead.
  We eat the cookies don't want my milk put it on the win-
dowsill go back to playing we play Old Maid Go Fish Fifty-
two Pick-up Cynthia shows me her closet All her dresses hang
in individual plastic bags and all the bags have zippers on them.
They fill the whole closet. She has more dresses now than I ever
had in all my eight years put together, least it seems that way.
  These are just my school dresses, she says. My dress-up clothes
are in the hall closet.

Love to look in her closet, imagine that I have all those dresses   never have to wear the same one twice   like going to the store every day.

Those are all my school shoes, she says.

A whole shelf piled with shoe boxes. But she always wears the same shoes to school – black patent shoes   white angora cuffed socks. Her shoes are always shiny and new

But you only have one pair, I say.

No, she says. I have eleven pairs. They just all look alike. I wear a different pair each day.

Rustling sound in the hall. Shiny robe   Cynthia's mother wandering to the bathroom   holds a glass of whiskey in her hand   lives in her bedroom   never comes out when I'm here doesn't say hello on her way back from the bathroom.

It's almost time to go when Cynthia suddenly announces she has a surprise   asks me to guess   can't guess   guess anyway   an elephant   an airplane ride   a trip to Zanzibar

A DOLL! she screams. Jumps up and down.

Mrs. Pearls comes running. What're you doing to her? she says to me.

Rachel didn't do anything, Cynthia says

I see she didn't drink her milk, Mrs. Pearls says, eyes pointing to the milk glass on the windowsill. Too many starving children in this town – drink that milk

Take a deep breath. Thought my mother was the only one knew about the starving children – but the ones she knows about are in Europe so maybe that's different

Mrs. Pearls marches her tall self over to the milk   brings it over   white milk dribbles on her hand

Drink this, she says

Don't make her, please, Cynthia begs

I take the glass. The glass is *hot*. The radiator sizzles on and I realize the glass has been sitting over the radiator for the whole time I've been here. I'm not thirsty   isn't fair   when Alice drank something there was a sign telling her to DRINK ME   and she wanted to   tip the glass to my mouth   thick taste   sour smell   don't want it   never will

Drink it, Mrs. Pearls says.

She stands with hands on hips tapping foot   she's not going to leave till I drink the whole thing   Cynthia should have warned me   I do drink it   eyes closed   don't breathe   my stomach feels as if boxing gloves are smashing it

Rest of my time there is hazy. I hold my stomach feeling sickness gurgle inside me   only a question of when not will I   Cynthia comes back in her room with a large doll   larger than my Alice doll, but with the same face. This is a doll made by the very famous designer, Madame Alexander, she tells me.

She holds it out for me to look at   can't take it   two hands on my stomach   the doll swings before me in Cynthia's arms   golden hair in a bun   dressed as a ballerina   tutu   toe shoes

ISN'T SHE BEAUTIFUL? Cynthia asks. ISN'T SHE THE MOST BEAUTIFUL DOLL YOU EVER SAW? MY FATHER BROUGHT IT OVER WHEN HE VISITED. IT COST A LOT OF MONEY

Stand there swaying   holding my stomach   sour milk in my throat   watching the most beautiful doll I've ever seen rock before me   silver tutu   better than Alice   glittery toe shoes   better than Alice   I want the tutu   better than Alice

Near the door I sit on the rug and tie up my brown oxfords and tiptoe over to the closet   my coat has fallen to the floor in a heap   put it on   knot my gray wool babushka under my chin   not like Cynthia's rabbit fur ear warmers.

Bye, Cynthia says.

She's holding her ballerina doll by the arm and I want to scream at her to hold it right   but my voice has gone somewhere inside me   and I rush out of the apartment. Into the elevator   I'm gonna be sick   I'm gonna be sick   I'm gonna be sick   look at the elevator operator   wears a hat with a chin strap   he doesn't seem as if he'll be happy if it happens here   lobby floor rush out   it's gonna happen   cold air hits my face   throw up in a stone flower pot with a bristly bush   no leaves.

*

Dinner is late. Hank and I are sitting on the beige leather

couches   you can see the dirt creases in the leather. He's on one couch because I don't like to sit near him and besides he's worn his White Sox sweatshirt every day this week and he doesn't smell too good. It's all wrinkled because he kept pulling it out of the dirty clothes hamper

We're having lamb stew, Hank mumbles.

Throat gags   What's that? I ask.

He gets a crooked grin on his mouth. It's pieces of Bo Peep's sheep hacked into chunks with lots of vegetables like turnips and rotten potatoes that that have their eyes poked out.

I grab my stomach   No way can I eat dinner.

Hank is reading a Superman comic and I'm reading a Little Lulu   We're both going through the comics for the third time   stacks of comics in the kitchen   but we can't go in.

A few minutes before my father came home from work   left his briefcase on the dining room floor.

DON'T YOU COME IN HERE, my mother shouted to Hank and me

They're shouting about money, Hank says. There's never enough of it. It's all your fault. If I didn't have a sister, there'd be plenty of money.

Not my fault   turn the page so hard the paper rips   not my fault my father found the bill for the Alice doll   too much money   not enough money   not my fault

The voices come closer. My mother appears in the dining room   holding a dish towel. I saved for those dolls, she says. Every week I put something aside. Anyhow, you can't do anything about it – they can't be returned now.

My father goes past her. Pushes up his wire glasses and sweeps his arm down for his briefcase. Once in a blue moon you can buy her a doll – but it's ridiculous the money you've spent.

Hank and I flip through our comics. We don't look up as my father stamps upstairs. I hear the thud of the briefcase in the master bedroom.

Get washed up for dinner, my mother says. Pulls at the dishtowel   goes back to the kitchen   turns on the radio loud   another symphony fills the downstairs.

*

My mother stays up all night making whirring sounds in the kitchen.

For Christ's sake, my father yells. Come upstairs.

Lie in bed   wonder what he means by come upstairs. My mother sleeps in the front bedroom sometimes   and in the back bedroom sometimes. She says it's because she snores and doesn't want to wake my father and he says it's because he has to get up extra early in winter to shovel the coal in the furnace and doesn't want to wake my mother and then they change stories which doesn't make sense because my father doesn't snore and my mother doesn't shovel the coal. Lately she's been sleeping in the back bedroom all the time. She even had a phone put in there – black, like the one downstairs. I was hoping for a different color, like gold, but no luck.

Next morning I find my mother asleep at the kitchen table, head down on a mound of material   sewing machine in front of her   my Alice doll is lying naked next to a napkin holder.

Where's breakfast? I say.

Oh. Rachel! My mother rubs her face and then shushes me, putting her finger over her mouth.

Before they come down, she says. Come here.

I tiptoe over to her   feeling a secret growing between us. She holds up a piece of red velvet, sequins sewn all over it   shows me other pieces   silvery things   Money can't buy this, she says, tracing her finger around the edge of a sequin.

*

I invite Cynthia over special   call her on the phone from my mother's room which seems like calling from a different house   Come over, I whisper, I've got a surprise, you won't believe it.

Cynthia knocks on the door   reach up   turn the brass lock   we hug each other   in my house you don't have to take off your shoes   she's holding her ballerina doll   tug her along to the dining room

Alice is sitting on the table where I placed her a few minutes before   her golden hair covered with a silver ballerina's netting like the kind that's over the bun on Cynthia's doll   silver ballet shoes shimmer on her feet   tights with silver streaks run up her legs   disappear under   I close my eyes not believing what I see   open them   it's true   red velvet tutu   red velvet cape spotted with sequins.

Where did you buy that? Cynthia says. It's beautiful. She rubs the netting on her ballerina doll's skirt.

I grin till I'm sure my back teeth show. I didn't buy it, silly. It's my Alice doll. My mother made the clothes. She stayed up all night and sewed the outfit. Money can't buy it.

Cynthia gets a frown on her face   clutches her doll to her chest   eyes dart around   she has big eyes and black circles under them   her eyes are looking for a place to hide   don't find any-place   she closes them and large drops of water big as dimes pop out

She stands there crying for a long time   when she cries no sound comes out   only shaking   shoulders mostly   when I cry big screams bounce out of me   land everywhere   makes my mother crazy   Cynthia hugs her doll   rocks back and forth   then she's finished doesn't say goodbye   just walks to the door   when it doesn't open she waits there   I reach up and turn the lock. I stand by the window watching her walk all the way to the corner and cross in the white lines   and somehow I get the feeling that I will never play with her again.

I leave Alice sitting on the table all day till my mother yells at me to get her off, we've got to set the table for dinner. I lift her down   can't help liking the red outfit but I carry her around the waist, swinging my arm   hoping I hit her head on the wall   knowing she's too big to flush down the toilet   not really wanting too   but not being able to be as pleased with her as I thought I'd be   not being able to pretend she's on a stage leap-ing and twirling   and what good is a doll if you can't pretend? No good. I put her in her special place at the foot of the bed   leave her standing with her arms outstretched   waiting to dance.

*

Sometimes my mother and I make a special trip downtown not
to the Art Institute   not to go to my father's law office   not to
shop or eat lunch   special trip to Marshall Field's
   Fifth floor
             doll room
   Dolls of all nations
             antique dolls in frilly dresses
   Dolls with porcelain faces and chipped noses
   Dolls in display cases with special temperature so they
won't wilt.
   A table filled with Storybook dolls propped up at an angle
in cardboard boxes with cellophane windows.
We wander through the room, hand in hand, stopping at almost
every doll, looking at it, admiring its ruffly dress or real eyelashes.
Look at how her nails are painted, my mother says.
   Sometimes we spend two hours in the doll room   longer than
we do in a gallery at the Art Institute   we rest on a bench and
do another round of the room
   we only go sometimes
                 when my mother feels like it
                 never when I do
   we only go sometimes
                 and we never tell my father.

Birthday Girl

THE ANCIENT MAN who lived down the block had the same birthday as mine. A man born in the 1800s was like my twin. These were impressive facts to me even as a tiny child. He was pale with wispy hair, and he hid inside the cocoon of his bathrobe. His wife wore street clothes, swept the walk and set Mr. Goldberg on the porch in his robe when it was sunny out. It did get sunny, even in Chicago in the 1950s where cars already parked nose to tail on our quiet block, and the last horse in the city that was not recreational stood near the church and synagogue, attached to a cart and a nosebag, waiting for his owner who peddled pots and pans door to door to come back and say "Gee up" and take him home. "A real throwback," my mother always said as the horse and cart passed by.

The morning of my fourth birthday I decided Mr. Goldberg must be lonely. After all, it was his birthday too, and he probably wasn't going to have a party. I put on my ugly brown robe inherited from my brother. It was the only robe I had, and my brother and I were instructed to put on our robes if we were going to walk around. The robe's hem made a good dust mop. "You'll grow into it," my mother said. The way I was supposed to grow into the dreaded camel's hair coat inherited from one of my boy cousins. The sleeve ends of the coat hit me at my knuckles, and my mother had to move the buttons way over. All she could see were those buttons. "Real leather," she exclaimed. They were dome-shaped with cracks in them. I put that coat on and felt geographically misplaced. No one could see me inside it, it was so huge. An observer saw a tan coat walking around with a thick wool babushka knotted double under an unseen chin. Not even its association with camels, which I loved to see at the zoo, could convince me that the coat had worth. Someone was kind enough to tell me that it buttoned on the wrong side for it to be a girl coat. To my complaints, my mother said, "It keeps you warm, that's the important thing."

Now, in the midst of summer, I didn't have to worry about warmth. It was steamy that morning when I slipped outside with the sash of the bathrobe snaking after me. It was so early our empty glass bottles were still in front, set out the night before for the Bowman milkman to exchange at dawn.

I walked down the street toward the Goldbergs. When I got to their front stoop, I screamed out, "MR. GOLDBERG, HAPPY BIRTHDAY!" My voice carried inside because their front door was already open, letting in the warm air through the screen.

"Rachel, what are you doing out there in your nightclothes?" Plump Mrs. Goldberg peered down at me. She was wearing a peek-a-boo blouse with glass buttons.

I shrugged, pushing my hair out of my face. I hadn't put the bobby pins in the way my mother did every morning. "I just want to wish Mr. Goldberg happy birthday," I said.

"Well, sit down on the step, child, and I'll get him."

She was gone a long time. A musty smell from inside seeped out – it was like the smell in our basement. When she returned, she came outside and handed me a huge sweetroll dripping with frosting, a much larger portion than I was allowed at home. We didn't ever have individual sweetrolls, but sometimes we had coffee cake, started at Sunday breakfast, what my mother called "a nosh," meant to last all day. As I plugged the sweetroll into my mouth, Mr. Goldberg shuffled onto the small front porch and sat in the rocker. The straw seat crunched when he made contact. "Happy birthday, Mr. Goldberg," I said, my mouth stuffed. "Are you having a cake later?"

Not too much more time went by before I saw my father of all people coming toward us. He had on jeans and a shirt that wasn't tucked in and his leather sandals that were so old his huge toes had formed depressions in the bottoms. He must have jumped out of bed about one second before. I never saw my father go outside the house without a tie on unless we were visiting relatives in the country.

"We'll just go home now," he said. "We're really sorry about this." He looked at Mrs. Goldberg. Mr. Goldberg had his eyes closed.

"But I haven't finished my roll," I wailed.

"You can take it home." Before I could explain anything, he swooped me up and with his hand went BOOM on my rear end, which my mother called derriere and my brother called butt. Right at that moment whatever it was called was hurting. BOOM BOOM BOOM and so it went all the way home. I was being carried under my father's arm. By the time he deposited me in the living room I was crying hard and my sweetroll was soggy.

"What is that she's eating?" my mother asked, running toward me. She took the remains of the roll out of my hand. "Rachel, stop crying now," she commanded, stooping down. "Just look at her." She hugged me and I cried harder. "Little girls do not sneak out of the house at six in the morning. My god, we didn't even know you were gone. What were you doing?" She frowned at me. Her black hair with the silver streaks was still in its long night braid.

"I was just . . . " I looked at my father and began crying harder. "Just trying to wish Mr. Goldberg happy birthday."

All this time my mother's friend Ruth was watching from the couch where she had been asleep. She pushed up her slip strap and smoothed down her curly hair. I wondered why she didn't have to put on her robe. Like my mother, she was a ceramic artist, and they often worked together firing pieces in the kiln. She had stayed over, not an unusual occurrence. "Rachel, you gave your parents a real scare," she said. "You're lucky to live in this lovely home with a mother and father. I should know. I came from a broken home."

"Will you look at this child," my mother said. She picked me up and took me to the back bathroom and washed my face. Then she sat me on a stool in the kitchen. My father and mother stared at me. "You've got to promise that you won't sneak out of the house again," my father said.

"I wasn't sneaking," I answered.

"Promise."

"I promise," I mumbled. "I was just . . . "

"No justs," my father said.

"He's right," my mother chimed in.

I tried to squint a mean look at her for going over to his side, but I could only make my bottom lip jut out.

"This is serious business, young lady," my father said. He was getting in what my mother called the last word.

Later that day my brother got to gloat about how much trouble I had gotten into on my birthday. His birthday was in winter, when the milk left outside formed a crust of ice, and it was so cold he would never think of sneaking out at six in the morning. My birthday present was a white cotton robe scattered with butterflies, store-bought, which was good, an aunt of mine later remarked. My mother had a reputation for sewing things crooked, buttons that stretched longingly for the buttonholes, and shirt pockets tipping over, spilling their contents. I loved my butterfly robe, and wore it as much as I could, though I never wore it outside. I watched with relief as my mother folded the brown robe and tucked it away until she could think of who to give it to. Some child-victim in our family would be able to wear it, if not now, later.

*

One summer my mother wanted to make me a birthday party. When she asked me for the names of friends to invite, I said there was only one person, Martin. Martin was a painter, an artist friend of my parents, and he lived next door in the basement. He had a loud laugh that my mother called a cackle, and, at the age of five, I was in love with him.

Martin came to my two-cupcake party on the screened back porch. He was wearing a flowery shirt. Unlike my father, he never wore a tie. My mother said, "I think I'll call Ruth and see if she wants to go shopping." That was probably wise since there were only two cakes. Each cake had a miniature candle planted in the middle, and Martin let me light them. "You have to sing," I told him.

"What do I sing?" he asked.

"You know. 'Happy Birthday.' "

"I forget the words."

"Mar-tin!"

"Okay. Come whisper them to me."

I climbed off the bench and went to his side and whispered the words in his ear. Then I went back around.

He sang "Happy Birthday" moving his lips, but no words came out.

"Louder," I said.

He opened his mouth wider and gestured with his arms. Before I could get angry at him, I started laughing.

"All finished," he said. You can make a wish."

After I blew out the candles, he asked me what I had wished. I told him I wanted to marry him.

"But I'm twenty years older than you."

"That's okay," I said.

"No, it's not okay." When he saw how disappointed I looked, he said he would think about it.

"We'll wait till you're grown up, and if you still feel the same way, we'll talk it over. Okay, kiddo?"

Somehow he got me to agree to that. We finished our cupcakes and sipped our lemonade from my father's special cone-shaped beer glasses. Then he took me next door and showed me his paintings. They were all of clocks, their insides bursting out, springs, screws exploding on the canvas. When I left to go home, he told me I was the prettiest birthday girl ever, and I think I smiled for the next month solid.

*

It was the summer of my ninth birthday and my parents' artist friends had banded together and made colorful gauze decorations for a backyard party. There were giant wire and gauze butterflies strung on lines over the yard. It was a beautiful day, magical with the decorations that floated above us. My friends from the neighborhood were there. My mother wore a sunsuit to bring out her freckles, and ruffled her fingers through her short hair. Less than a year before we had visited her sister in Los Angeles where she had chopped off her thick black hair, leaving it like a cap against her head. The artists were inside on the screened porch, laughing, drinking, and smiling out at the children's party, pleased with their creation.

Much later I lay on the couch in the dim, shade-drawn living room surrounded by little presents my friends had brought. My head hurt and I was as hot as our coal furnace in winter. I fingered the plastic pop beads, trying to make a bracelet, but it was hard to pop them together. Someone came to the door. My mother's friend Ruth. She was out walking her Borzoi dog Prince Andrei, and thought she'd come over. She and my mother hugged and sat down in chairs opposite me. Ruth was newly divorced, and she often talked to my mother about her problems. Prince Andrei sat at her feet, shaking his head, making his collar tags rattle.

"Can I pet him?" I called from the couch.

"Sure," Ruth said. "Come over here. I have a present for my birthday girl."

As I sat up, my whole body ached and shooting pains danced up and down my arms and legs. "I don't feel good," I said.

"She has a bad headache," my mother explained. "Too much sun and cake and ice cream."

I slid off the couch, and instead of standing, my legs collapsed under me like an umbrella closing.

When I woke up next I was lying in my bed upstairs and the doctor was examining me. "I want to pet Prince Andrei," I said.

"There'll be plenty of time for that soon enough," she said, pushing the stethoscope over my heart. "I want you to wiggle your fingers for me."

It was at that moment I realized that I couldn't move my arms or legs. I didn't know how to make them work any more. For a whole week people came and went from my bedroom. My father, who hadn't been around the house as much, took off time from his job as a lawyer, and carried me to the bathroom several times a day. Ruth sat watch with my parents, spelling my mother so she could nap. Once she brought Prince Andrei to see me. His tall body loomed in the shadows of my room, and later I thought his visit had been a dream. I knew I was really sick. Never did my brother or I stay upstairs when we were sick – we always lay on the couch in the living room. The words paralyzed and polio drifted in from the hallway. I knew about polio. It was the illness that struck in summer, during the very time of my birthday. I thought about all the icy water I had guzzled after racing a friend down the block, and how I had gone swimming after eating a big lunch – the sure ways to contract polio.

For one week I lay frozen in bed, too sick to know how worried everyone was. Then one morning I woke up and concentrated hard and was able to wiggle my little finger. It felt like ice cracking inside. Gradually my whole body felt like ice cracking, and by the time my mother had me in a taxi, an unheard-of luxury, to go to the doctor, I was moving all my parts. "Walk across the room," the doctor said, and I walked to her on unsteady feet, but made it without crumbling.

Later that year, long after my birthday had scared my parents enough to stand over my bed arms entwined, Ruth stopped coming over to our house. I begged for Prince Andrei to visit us again so I could pet the silky fur on his blade-thin body. All my mother said was, "We'll see" and gave me a far away look. I was to find out soon enough that Ruth would become my stepmother, after my parents' divorce which my mother thought was for the best and later regretted to the deepest corners of her soul.

The Sadie Hawkins Day Dance

RACHEL FIRST SAW her on the steps of the high school talking to some girls during a bomb scare. Someone mumbled that Barbara Jo must be the fattest girl in the sophomore class. There was giggling for a moment and Rachel was glad for once that *she* was thin, thin as a rail her father always said. Rachel was standing near the curb behind the group of girls while Barbara Jo told them how she was going to become a model. The man at the studio, she said, told me to come in Friday, that he likes my face – I have a widow's peak, you know. She bent her head and pushed up the hair from her forehead so everyone could see. Rachel stood on tiptoes so she could see too, and she touched her own forehead for a moment, and thought how her face was too long, and her nose didn't seem to set right when she saw it in the mirror.

*

Rachel lived close enough to the school to walk. She crossed over to the other side of the street so she didn't have to pass by the groups of students waiting for the bus. At home she sneaked in the door and went up the stairs, stepping on the side near the railing which was less worn and so it didn't creak as much.

Her mother was usually talking on the kitchen phone, and if she heard Rachel come home, she said, just a minute, Esther –

she was always talking to Aunt Esther – and then she yelled, Rachel is that you – knowing that it was. Rachel flinched and made a fist so her nails marked her palms, and debated whether to answer or not. She usually said, yeah, it's me, and dashed upstairs. If she didn't answer by the time she got to her room, her mother was at the bottom of the stairs screaming up to her, why don't you answer me when I ask a question, and Rachel stood by the full length mirror and listened to the shouting, holding her breath and feeling sick. When her mother finally stopped, she threw her books on the bed, and sat next to them at the foot facing the mirror where she saw herself running her fingers through her long brown hair pinned back with a barrette.

She tugged at her crinkly stretchy bobby socks, pulling them up again toward her knees, fixing the rubber band garters so they didn't show. This year the socks were pulled up. Last year they had been cuffed over in a tube around the ankle.

Sometimes she undressed and stared at her naked body, wondering when her tiny breasts would get large. One afternoon she even took her white cotton brassiere, which had concentric circle stitching around the cups, and stuffed it with the flowered handkerchiefs which she collected over the years at birthdays from Aunt Esther who wanted to make sure her niece grew up to be a lady. The handkerchiefs in the brassiere were uneven, but they did puff her out under the sweater.

*

One afternoon her brother yelled from the first floor, hey, Rachel, telephone for you. She shut her book, wondering who it was, and she went downstairs to the kitchen wall phone. Her brother said, some girl wants to talk to you. He lifted his unfinished bottle of Coca-Cola off the sink, and belched loudly behind her back as she went to the phone, and he laughed when she turned around and glared at him.

Hello, Rachel, the voice on the phone said. Yeah, she answered, waiting to see who it was. The voice said, this is Barbara Jo, we met yesterday on the steps by school. She sounded out of breath. She asked Rachel what the history lecture was about this morning – she had missed it. Rachel was surprised. She hadn't noticed they had the same lecture. She told her they had seen a movie about the Civil War, the one they show in every grade from sixth on, and Barbara Jo said, are you sure that was all, her voice accusing her of holding out. Rachel said, yes, and we're having a test next week. Oh, shit, Barbara Jo said, wouldn't you know old lady Nickles would do that. Rachel was silent. Mrs. Nickles was forty, and she had never thought of her as *old lady Nickles* before.

They were quiet for a moment and Rachel asked her if she was excited about Friday. Friday, why should I be, Barbara Jo asked, still with that faintly accusing voice. You know, Rachel said, that modeling job you were talking about. Oh, yeah, Barbara Jo said, oh, yeah, sure I'm excited – wouldn't you be . . . but I don't suppose *you* ever did anything like that. Then she asked about the exact day of the test. When Rachel told her, she said, well, I suppose I'll see you in school, and they hung up.

The following Friday Barbara Jo wasn't in history lecture and Rachel wondered if she really did go to the modeling job. She was standing by the auditorium. April Peterson, who was the most popular girl in the sophomore class, was across the hall talking to a girl Rachel didn't recognize. April had golden hair, and she always said, I'm just helping mother nature along, if anyone asked her if she bleached it. Once she had cornered Rachel, and in a solemn voice had said, *you should really have a perm to get rid of that string-mop hair of yours.* Another time she had come up to Rachel in the hall and told her, something's showing, you better get to the bathroom quick. Rachel had pushed through the crowds in the hall and walked through the swing doors of the bathroom which was full of smoke. She was certain she had her period and that it was showing through her dress. A great ink blot of blood. She snapped the stall door closed. She'd have to stay here till the bathroom cleared out and she could wash her dress. But when she looked, she found that she didn't have her period. Her slip was showing a little, that was all. She had sucked in air in small gobbles, furious at April, and relieved at the same time.

When April noticed her standing by the auditorium, Rachel turned and pretended to read a brass plaque on the wall: The War Dead – a list of this high school's graduates who had died in wars. But April approached her, saying, I hear you and that fat girl are friends, pretty good friends too. Rachel tensed inside. She had had lunch with Barbara Jo the day before, and she was going to her house for dinner tomorrow. She mumbled, no, not really, keeping her eyes on the names before her. April laughed aloud. Rachel didn't turn around until the sound from the tiny silver taps on the bottom of April's shoes had disappeared down the stairs.

*

The next afternoon Rachel told her mother she had been invited out for dinner. Her mother was browning frozen fillet of sole at the stove, and she said, why didn't you let me know sooner, we were going to have an early dinner because your father called – he's in town and he's coming over around eight. Rachel held her breath, wondering how she would get out of this one. Everything depended on saying the right thing. Hank came in the kitchen and said, she's going over to the fat girl's house, the fat girl's house, and her mother said, goddamnit, stop acting like you're ten. He was sixteen, but he did act like ten a lot, Rachel thought, wishing her brother would drop dead. When he had painted their garage last summer, he had climbed to the top and slapped the word SHIT on the tar roof, large enough for anyone down the block to see. Well, I want to go, she said, trying to forget that her father was coming over. I'll be back in time, she added, seeing her mother frown. Well, you better, she said, I'm not going to be left here to entertain him alone – he wants to see you.

She walked the three blocks to Barbara Jo's and waited in the dark hallway. The buzzer blurted out and she jumped a little and opened the heavy glass door. Barbara Jo was leaning over the railing of the second landing. She asked Rachel if anything was exciting, and Rachel shrugged her shoulders and Barbara Jo said, god, there must be something, and Rachel squirmed under her stare that wouldn't let up.

They went into Barbara Jo's room. It was filled with dolls. This is my collection, they're from all over the world, she said. She lifted one down, touching a lace head covering, saying, this is a mantilla, I have a real one too. My grandparents go to Spain every year and they brought it back for me – I'll probably go with them next year. She paused, watching Rachel for a reaction. Rachel said, I . . . uh, have dolls too, but they're put away in the attic. Oh, I don't *play* with them, she said, they're just to look at. There was a poster of Johnny Mathis hanging over the radiator and Barbara Jo informed her that she had his autograph. Really, Rachel said. She thought he must be a singer because there was a microphone in the picture, but she wouldn't have recognized his voice if she heard it on the radio.

They sat in her room for another while, talking about school. Barbara Jo showed her all her new clothes – even her new brassieres, which had three hooks in back. She told Rachel it was a pity she didn't have more up front, and Rachel said, oh well, it's not so bad. She would fill out sometime, she thought. Barbara Jo's breasts were huge – they made her look as if she would topple over at any minute. She smiled at the thought, and Barbara Jo asked her what she was grinning at. You know, if we're going to be friends, we can't have secrets. Friends don't have secrets.

*

They ate cold tuna fish for dinner. Barbara Jo's mother didn't get home from work till midnight, and they didn't have any other food that Barbara Jo knew how to make. When it was time to go, Barbara Jo asked why she had to leave so soon. Rachel didn't want to tell her, but she finally said because her father was coming to visit, and Barbara Jo asked her what she meant. She told her that her parents were divorced, hearing the word divorce at a distance, like an echo.

Barbara Jo's form blocked the door like a fence. She wanted to know everything, Rachel guessed, from the excited, curious look on her face. She stood, twisting the ends of her long straight hair, suddenly asking Barbara Jo, where's *your* father. Her friend's mouth opened. Why . . . why do you want to know. Rachel shrugged, but now she was curious. Well, she said, why don't you answer me. My father's dead, Barbara Jo told her. He died when I was five. He loved me more than anyone. She started to cry, and Rachel put out her arm toward her, watching her skin shiver as Barbara Jo cried harder. Although she was sorry Barbara Jo was crying, she was secretly pleased that a question she had asked could have such a strong effect. She went home, almost looking forward to seeing her father, only to find he hadn't shown up at all. Her brother was watching TV and he only let her sit in the room if she were eight feet away, so she sat near the doorway, staring at the flickering cowboy on the screen, wondering why her father hadn't visited when he said he would.

*

In the next few weeks, she and Barbara Jo became close friends. They saw each other every day, usually walking home to Rachel's house, which was closer to school. They called each other on the telephone and talked for two hours sometimes, and Barbara Jo showed Rachel how to fix her hair, like a model, she said. Rachel loved to watch her put on make-up. She used a special make-up mirror her mother had given her for her birthday, and she let Rachel hand her each tube and bottle as she needed them. She curled her eyelashes with a press and tweezed her eyebrows, then drew them in again in a thin ellipse. She often switched the lighting on the mirror, saying, this is how I would look in an office, this is how I would look in candlelight, and Rachel tried to see the difference. She was amazed at Barbara Jo's endless supply of clothes – drawers full of sweaters and a closet stuffed so she could never find what she wanted.

One afternoon while they were sitting and watching TV, Barbara Jo said, that Jeffery Atkins, he's such a creep, and that Simmons guy, I bet he doesn't even know where babies come from. Then she stood up and went to her kitchen for more popcorn. She came back with her cheeks ballooning out, and sat down on the floor next to Rachel, telling her that in actual fact, most of the guys in school were real creeps, didn't she agree. She didn't wait for her to answer, but said, well, all the guys are creeps except one. Who, Rachel asked. Barbara Jo smirked, saying, *Todd*. Todd Everest, who's on the football team, Rachel asked. She nodded, and said, he came over last night – he was here when I talked to you on the phone.

Rachel stared at her. He comes over a lot, Barbara Jo continued, only I promised him I wouldn't tell anyone – you're the first person and you better not blab.

Rachel said she wouldn't. She knew that Todd dated April Peterson, and she was confused about what Barbara Jo told her. She looked down at the floor wondering if a boy would ever come over to visit her, and if her mother would let her go out. Lots of boys came over to visit Hank. Her mother had once warned him that he better keep his friends away from his sister or he'd be in trouble.

*

In the winter she and Barbara Jo sat in front of the woodburning fire that Rachel's mother started when the furnace wasn't adequate. Now every time they talked, Barbara Jo mentioned Todd, how he came over almost every night and left just before her mother got home at midnight. She was sitting in front of the fire one afternoon polishing her nails and Rachel was reading. He kisses me, she said, watching Rachel, who looked up saying, oh really, I thought he was pinned to April. Barbara Jo wrinkled up her face and said, of course he is silly, but he says she *won't put out*. Rachel thought she knew what Barbara Jo meant, but she wasn't sure, so she said, why won't she. Barbara Jo ignored her question, blowing on her nails. She said that sometimes – and she got that smirk on her face that always made Rachel uncomfortable – sometimes we lay down on the bed, *in the dark*. She added *in the dark* as a kind of bonus. Rachel waited for more, but Barbara Jo said, why don't we make a sandwich or something, and then I have to go home.

*

It's not really Sadie Hawkins Day, Barbara Jo told Rachel, but they're calling the dance that anyway. Everything is in reverse –

when you get there, you're supposed to ask guys to dance. Barbara Jo asked her if she were going to invite someone, and Rachel shook her head. She couldn't think of anyone she dared to ask. Well, we can go, Barbara Jo said, 'cause it's not like a prom, you don't have to have a date.

They were over at Barbara Jo's where Rachel was spending the night, which she did several times a month, sleeping on the trundle bed that pulled out from Barbara Jo's. At midnight Barbara Jo turned off the light, and they waited in the dark for her mother to open the bedroom door and check to see that they were sleeping. After a few minutes they sat up and Barbara Jo lit a candle. Rachel wondered where Todd was – Barbara Jo had told her he came over almost every night. As if she read those thoughts, Barbara Jo said that Todd had gone away with his family for the weekend. Then she grinned and said that now they took off their clothes in bed. Even your underpants, Rachel asked. Of course, she said, how else do you think we do it. Rachel's heart was beating fast, and she didn't know if she should ask more or not, but Barbara Jo said, he puts it inside me and he said yesterday that he's afraid that I'll get a baby. Rachel didn't know what to say. Her mother had once screeched and screeched at her when she found her and the boy who lived down the block rolling around on the living room floor tickling each other. If you ever do that again, I'll kill you, she had said, dragging Rachel up and telling the boy to get out or I'll call the police. She had sent Rachel to her room, telling her it was dirty and to never let a boy do that again, and she made Rachel promise. Rachel asked Barbara Jo what it was like, and she said, oh, it's nice – one time he brought a friend and I did it with him too.

Rachel closed her eyes, knowing that deep down Barbara Jo was lying, like she did about everything, so she shouldn't think about what she had told her any more. She could see the bulky form under the covers next to her, and she finally went to sleep, listening to the steady asthmatic wheezing that plagued her friend.

*

The day of the Sadie Hawkins Day Dance she spent two hours in her room trying on almost everything she owned to see what she would wear. Nothing looked right. Finally she decided on a red wool dress. Her brother came to her room and said, the fat girl's here, and Rachel said, all right, and went downstairs. Her mother said, now you go right to Barbara Jo's after the dance and call me when you get there. She stood by the door to see them off, and waited, blocking it until Rachel knew she was supposed to kiss her goodbye which she hated to do, but her mother wasn't moving. She closed her eyes and whisked her mother's soft cheek with her lips and cringed inside. She wanted to be like Barbara Jo, who hugged her mother – she wished she could be good the way her mother wanted her to be.

The dance was held in the gym. When the live band began to play, the girls lined up on one side of the gym, behind the line for uniform inspection. They rushed across the floor, chasing boys, trying to catch someone. Rachel was pinned between two girls and one of them shoved her out of the way. She went over to the side where Barbara Jo was standing. I'm waiting for the snowball dance, she said to Rachel – I see you weren't too successful. I'm going to the bathroom, Rachel said, I'm not feeling well. She went through the gym doors and out into the silent halls, hearing the music and laughter in the distance. *How was the dance*, her mother would ask. *When I was your age, I had lots of boyfriends.* She wasn't going to dance, that was clear – she wanted to get Barbara Jo to leave as soon as possible.

Near the bathroom, someone yelled out, hey you, wait a minute. It was Denny Taylor whom Rachel recalled seeing around last year. He had a moustache now, and his hair was longer than when she had last seen him. She looked up at him baffled. What did he want with her? He had been a varsity letterman and she was positive he didn't know her. She didn't want to talk to anyone just now, and she sucked in her breath hoping it would hold back the tears she had been certain of a minute ago. He was talking to her, and she finally said, what. He said, weren't you listening – you women are all alike – you never listen. Rachel frowned. She didn't think of herself as a woman. Women were mothers or aunts – someone she vaguely knew she was going to be in a distant time. I'm . . . I'm sorry, she said. She was almost safe. The bathroom door was a foot away. But he stretched his arm across the door. Are you Barbara Jo's friend, he asked. She said, yeah, why. He said he and a buddy wanted to see her outside, they were in the parking lot. Who are you with, she asked. Todd, he said. Just tell her to come out to the parking lot. Rachel was silent. And *you* can come too, he said, peering inside her, it seemed, as he said it, tossing back his scraggly hair. As he walked away, he pointed his finger and said, hurry, we haven't got all night to wait.

So Barbara Jo knew Todd. Everything she had said was true, and here she hadn't believed it. Rachel went back in the gym, which was now dimly lit, and walked around the edges by the stall bars till she found Barbara Jo by the punch bowl sipping from a paper cup with her little finger arched. When she told her about Todd wanting to see her, she said, o-h-h, and set down her cup. Let's go, you come too, please, she said, and Rachel told her that Denny had said she should anyway. Before she could decide whether she should or not, they were outside in the chilly spring air and Barbara Jo was hurrying ahead to a parked car near the fence.

Then she stopped, saying, do you like Denny, I think he's good looking. Rachel said, yeah, I guess, but I don't really know him. Well, try to keep him company or something, Barbara Jo said, 'cause Todd and me, we'll probably, you know . . .

They got into the car, Rachel in the back with Denny, who said, well, I'm glad to see you, and he pushed his cigarette into the little metal tray and snapped it shut and said, let's go. Todd turned and smiled and put his arm over the back of the seat and snaked it around Barbara Jo, pulling her toward him. All Rachel could think was that she hadn't believed her, and it was all true about Todd.

They ended up going to Barbara Jo's house after driving around for a while. Rachel couldn't think of anything to say to Denny after she had asked him what year he was in and he said he dropped out of school. *Don't be friends with dumb kids.* If her mother's rule from long ago still held true, she shouldn't even be talking to Denny.

When they got to Barbara Jo's, she and Denny trailed behind, and when they walked in, only the hall light was on, and the bedroom door was shut. Rachel stood in the living room. She had to keep him company. He asked her what kind of music she liked. He had found the radio in the dim light and was kneeling down by it, waiting for her answer. She couldn't think of any thing to say, so she said, most anything. It didn't matter. All she wanted was for Barbara Jo to hurry up. Well, aren't you going to sit down, he asked. He stood waiting. She said down in a chair, hoping he would sit across the room. She didn't care anymore what was going on in the bedroom – she only wanted them to hurry.

He came over and sat on the arm of her chair, and pulled a paper bag from his jacket and asked her if she wanted a sip. A sip of what, she asked, and he laughed. How the fuck old are you, he said nonchalantly, taking a sip himself.

She stared ahead, pretending not to have heard. He had used the worst swear word on earth: *boys only did that when they thought girls were cheap*, her mother had said. Boys weren't supposed to swear when they were around you. They were supposed to be polite, and if they weren't, you knew what they were thinking about you.

How old are you, he said again. Fourteen, she mumbled, but I'll be fifteen in two months. Fourteen, he said, laughing again. Why you little angel. She had never thought of herself as a little angel before and she was embarrassed. Somehow it was a compliment, but she wasn't sure if she should still be angry for him saying the word *fuck*, or whether that was over and done with. He put the paper sack in her hand and said that she should take one drink and if she didn't like it that was okay. She said, no, she didn't think she wanted to, she didn't like liquor, she had tasted it plenty of times and it smelled bad. He laughed again. It was true enough. She had tasted it plenty of times when her father had given her drinks from his glass, which angered her mother and caused huge arguments. Sometimes she had taken so many sips she had felt dizzy from it.

His leg flopped down on her lap and he said, excuse me, only he didn't take it off. Her body became still, like the statue game she had played as a child. She breathed very slowly, as if any indication of her breathing would remind him that she was alive. Your friend is real nice, he said, pointing to the bedroom, aren't you going to be nice too, nice to *me*. She smelled whisky float down at her. She wanted to cry out, Barbara Jo, Barbara Jo, but she didn't. She sat and waited, hearing the static on the radio for the first time.

He eased down into her chair and she moved over, sitting on the edge and he said, oh angel, what's wrong, did I scare you, and he laughed again. Why did he laugh so much. He put his hands on her shoulders, and then – she knew it was because she didn't move – he began playing with the neckline of her dress – running his finger along it, his nail touching her skin. he wants me to be *nice*, she thought. Barbara Jo said to keep him *company*. Her body was a part of the chair, couldn't he tell that, why did he keep on.

Suddenly he grabbed her around the waist and they were down on the floor, and she struggled, but his body was heavy on her. She could hardly breathe, and he kept saying, you little bitch, you little bitch. The more he said it, the angrier she got and she pounded her fists against him whenever her hand got free. She heard the sound of clinking metal. His belt buckle. *He was taking down his pants*. She screamed. She finally found the scream somewhere inside her. She screamed so loud everything stopped for a second and there was only the scream. A door opened in the distance, and at the same time Denny reached under her dress and ripped at her underpants. At first his fingers jabbed at her, and she gasped, no. Then she felt something else that was hard trying fiercely to get inside her. *The man places his penis inside the woman's vagina.* Her mother's calm explanation of how babies were made scooted across her memory, and she thought, he's trying to do that to me, only it's hard, Barbara Jo never told me it was hard. She screamed again, and Denny said, try to like it, angel, and she pushed him, but he didn't budge.

Get the hell away from her. Suddenly Barbara Jo was there, and she kicked at Denny, and Todd was saying, as he grabbed at him, hey man, you can go to jail for this. She lay on the floor staring up at the plaster swirls in the ceiling, hearing Denny cursing Barbara Jo out for kicking him. She hurt all over.

I want to go home, she said, looking at Barbara Jo, whose blouse was half-buttoned. Barbara Jo's make-up was smeared and the curls which she had worked so hard at were smashed against her head. Denny was talking with Todd. They were joking about something, and Rachel said again, I want to go home.

I thought you had a friend who would do it, Denny said. You promised. Rachel looked at her, holding her breath, waiting for her to deny it, but Barbara Jo said, shut up, damn it. She wouldn't look at Rachel. Todd said, baby, let's go back in the bedroom – your mother might come home early or something. Barbara Jo said, can't you see she's upset, and Todd said, yeah, but she's okay, he didn't rape her or anything. Barbara Jo looked at her and said, he didn't, did he, and Rachel started crying. It hurt so much between her legs. Then she said, no I don't think so.

Barbara Jo helped her to the bathroom and told her to straighten up and they would take her home, in five minutes, no longer. She saw her tangled hair in the mirror and reached for a comb. She heard the bedroom door slam, and then laughter, coming muted through the wall. It felt numb where he had jabbed her. It had never felt numb there before.

She stayed in the bathroom until she heard the bedroom door open. It must have been a half-hour later. She walked out in the hall and waited. The three of them came out of the bedroom, with Barbara Jo giggling in a silly, drunken voice that Rachel now hated. She wanted to get away, never see her again. She let boys do all those things to her, and she had planned it with Denny. Denny looked at her, sneering, taking time buckling his belt. He grabbed Barbara Jo by the neck and kissed her on the cheek. She blushed and then turned from him, saying to Rachel, hey, I'm sorry about what happened. I thought you could handle it. She felt the three of them watching her. Todd was smiling –

they were amused. She shrugged and said, I just want to go home, take me home.

Someone turn off the radio, Barbara Jo said. She had taken out a lipstick container which had a mirror attached and was puckering her lips into it. Denny went over to the radio. There was slow music playing. Hey, you want to dance, anyone, and he held an imaginary partner and circled around the room. Oh brother, Todd said. Rachel stood by the door, wishing they could leave. Suddenly Denny circled by her, grabbing her hand, saying, wanna dance, and he jerked her across the room. Her body flopped after him, and she said, stop it. Hey, cut the crap, Barbara Jo said. Rachel pulled away from him and went over to the door. Will you turn off the damn radio, Barbara Jo yelled. Todd, make him hurry up. Rachel opened the door quietly and closed it behind her. She would walk home. She had somehow forgotten she was so close by. She ran down the stairs before they could realize that she had left.

When she got home, she heard her mother talking on the phone, and she didn't know what she would do if she had to explain a lot. I'm home, Mom, she said, darting in the kitchen so her mother could see her in real life. I decided not to stay overnight at Barbara Jo's. Then she darted out again and went upstairs, expecting to be called back down, but for once nothing happened.

*

Over the weekend she stayed around the house, helping her mother in the kitchen and garden. She reached over to her mother at the table and hugged her for a moment. She wanted to tell her what had happened to her. She wanted to throw her arms around her and cry and have her mother say that it would be all right. Barbara Jo didn't phone her, and Rachel didn't want to talk to her anyway. When she saw her in school, she would ignore her.

But Barbara Jo wasn't in school all week. When Rachel finally tried to call her, there was no answer. When she came home on Friday, Hank and her mother were in the living room. Guess what, her brother said. That fat girl's gone and got herself pregnant. Rachel frowned. What was he talking about. How did he know. I heard from some of the parents, her mother said. She's been having boys over to her apartment for the last few months. She's a real slut. I knew you shouldn't be hanging around with older girls. She's the same age as me, Rachel said. She skipped a grade in grammar school like I did.

Her mother stood. I don't give a damn how old she is, she screamed, *she's a slut*, and I hope to god that you didn't do those things they say she did. I hope you'll never let a boy do those things to you.

The voice bounced at her and she ducked involuntarily. Are you listening to me, the voice said. Yes, Rachel answered. Hank was grinning from his chair. She closed her eyes. Now she couldn't tell her mother anything. *Mama, I was scared to death and his body was so heavy.* If she told her, her mother would say she had been doing those bad things, even though she hadn't meant to. But Denny had touched her *there*, and she felt a twinge between her legs. She could still feel him trying to get at her. *He wanted to rip me open, Mama.*

Then her mother said she was going to call Barbara Jo's mother, to tell her how sorry she was for her. No, please don't do that, Rachel said, no, please don't, and she followed her to the kitchen and watched as she dialed Mrs. Thompson's work number, which she had somehow gotten. But she hung up soon, saying in a flat, disappointed voice, she doesn't work there anymore, she quit this morning. They must have moved, she added. It's no wonder. What a disgrace.

Rachel went into the living room and turned on the television. It was an advanced French lesson on the educational channel. She stared at it, saying some of the sentences. *Ses valises sont ici, mais sa malle est encore à la gare.* That girlfriend of yours is sure fat, Hank said, and now she's gonna be even fatter. He laughed, and she lunged at him, screaming, shut up, bastard, and she punched out at him and kicked him. He threw her across the room and she crashed into the couch. You filthy ass, she said. It was the first time she had used swear words out loud at him, and she was surprised at how easy it was. She wouldn't ever tell

Hank and her mother that she hated Barbara Jo – they would want to know why.

*

A few weeks later Rachel saw Barbara Jo standing by a cosmetics counter in Marshall Field's. Barbara Jo was saying to the salesclerk, see, I have a widow's peak, and she bent her head and pushed back her hair to show her. Rachel froze, then turned and walked quickly away, hoping Barbara Jo didn't see her.

When she got home, she hurried to her room, avoiding Hank who was watching TV. She looked in her mirror, and she thought that her breasts were getting a little fuller, for which she was grateful. Then she pushed up the hair on her forehead to check for what Barbara Jo considered the ultimate beauty mark. Maybe she had gotten one since the last time she looked. It was no use. There wasn't a widow's peak to be seen. She had counted on it being there, and she sat down on her bed, hating Barbara Jo even more, still feeling the hairline by her forehead.

She fell asleep and was awakened after a while by Hank's yelling from downstairs. She went to her bedroom door. What, she yelled back. He said that it was the telephone, for her. She went slowly down to the first floor. It's that fat pig of a girlfriend, he said, she's on the phone. He pinched his nose and stuck out his tongue. She didn't want to talk to her, and at the same time she was glad that her mother wasn't home. Hank, tell her I'm not here, *please*. He shook his head. I don't think she'll be able to understand me, he said. Rachel was certain he was going to make some remark about Barbara Jo's ear being so fat she couldn't hear. When she asked for you, he continued, I could hardly understand her at first she was crying so hard. With that, he went back to watch TV.

She walked into the kitchen and found the receiver which he had put behind the toaster. Hello, she said, in a monotone voice. Rachel, Barbara Jo said, oh Rachel. She coughed. I saw you earlier, Rachel said, by the cosmetics counter. Really, Barbara Jo said, I didn't see you. Rachel was positive from her voice that she had seen her. Well, what do you want, Rachel asked. Oh,

Barbara Jo gasped, oh, and she began to cry. Rachel didn't say anything. Please listen, Barbara Jo pleaded. She was crying harder. Then she said, I lost it, I lost the baby. Huh, Rachel said, what do you mean. You can't lose babies before they're born. I did, Barbara Jo said, I did, it came out of me – it was awful, it hurt so much, and there was blood. And my mother was at work. Rachel was silent. She pulled at the oilcloth so hard she almost jerked it off the table. Oh Barbara Jo, she finally said, I didn't know it was like that. I'm sorry. And she cried too, listening to Barbara Jo's wheezing tear-filled voice tell her everything.

Family Meetings

AUNT ROSE'S BODY dimensions were solid and predictable, like a brick. Only her huge bosom pronounced her a woman in spite of herself. She couldn't hide it, no matter how much she wanted to. Her round front, carefully snared in a net of bones, always preceded her in life. It was a bosom so well reined in it didn't dare move when she walked, and when Miriam was hugged by her aunt, there was nothing soft about the experience. Aunt Rose was so self-conscious about the word "breast" that she banned it from her thoughts. Thinking about it might make her say it.

Dodging that one word was always a problem for her because of all the food in the world, she loved chicken the most, and of the chicken she was cursed to like the white meat only. A look of despair and greed played on her face at a restaurant – she had to ask directly for what she wanted. But on her turf the story was different. She was the one who controlled the platter of chicken, in pieces or whole. Her husband Newton always sat next to her and looked down at his plate as if something very sad had just happened. All the skin and muscles in his face hung down as if there were a magnet in his dish. He never carved the chicken, and he only spoke when someone asked him something. His face was foggy with whiskers. Rose didn't ask anybody for the piece of chicken she wanted at her own table. She got the whole breast without a syllable escaping from her mouth.

To go to Aunt Rose's when Miriam was six took a major shift of planets. Off came the grubby jeans and tattered sneakers. The skin was scrubbed with Ivory, the long hair untangled, and the complaints ignored. Her feet, disguised as sausages, were encased in her white Sunday-school-and-party socks which in turn were stuffed into her black patent shoes that she had to coat with Vaseline when she took them off to keep them from cracking like eggshells. Her head was declared missing under a wide-brimmed straw hat with a ribbon that was pinked at the end so it wouldn't unravel if she picked at it. In between the hat and shoes was her body, covered with a Kate Greenaway dress of polished cotton that always had a hidden pocket in it, which was the best thing about it, because most dresses didn't have pockets. Aunt Rose gave her a Kate Greenaway dress every year because she said Miriam's mother didn't know how to choose clothes properly. The outfit was decorated with a hankie pinned to her waist. It had sculpted edges made of organdy that burned your nose if you tried to use it. And in the magic pocket were the white cotton gloves that she would have to put on eventually that got dirty if she smiled the wrong way. The outfit was complete.

The family gathered each month at one sister's house or another's to hold a Family Meeting. The sisters had been known since their childhood as the Flower Girls: Violet, Miriam's mother; Rose, the oldest; Daisy, the fashion model; and Lily, the grammar school art teacher who could materialize a miniature papier-mâché village on demand. During the Christmas season Aunt Rose spent her time clucking on the phone because Lily was commissioned to make papier-mâché nativity scenes for people, not only in the privacy of their homes, but for churches even, where she was actually seen in public installing works of art. Christianity to Aunt Rose was like being served the neck and backbone of the chicken. She would die a thousand times when she heard that Lily spent the afternoon inside a church, and not only in the lobby, but in that dark place where they keep the cross and burn incense. Cavorting with Christians was like adding water to soup just before you serve it to make it go farther; taste suffers. Quality in life becomes vestigial, like the appendix.

Visiting Aunt Rose took preparation. At everyone else's house you could wear things that didn't match or that needed cleaning. But Aunt Rose demanded perfection even from the adults. The sisters put on their version of the dog. Which meant Miriam's mother wore a gray skirt with a white blouse that was free of the red ink that marked her life as a bookkeeper. Daisy always wore something that reminded everyone of a fancy nightgown; it was filmy and looked as if it were ready to sail whenever the parachute opened. Lily always chose something with large flowers on it – her sisters called them wallpaper dresses. Uncle Mort wore his usual suit. He was a clothing salesman and he like to be prepared in case a customer showed up. Newton wore a bow tie. Even when he was in the hospital once Miriam heard her mother say he wore his bow tie.

Aunt Rose's house bristled with bushes all around it. They were neatly trimmed bushes that were allowed to show a flower or two once in a while if they didn't make a commotion. Since Aunt Rose didn't work, she spent huge amounts of time in her yard trimming things and making them grow just so she could trim them. She always wore dark skirts and thick shoes with laces. She was the only one of the Flower Girls who didn't work any more because Newton had gotten his disability pension reinstated. How Newton had been disabled was a secret that never escaped the lips of the Flower Girls. They gave each other knowing glances when Newton was discussed, passing around their secret to each other, but no one on their outskirts, like nieces and nephews, ever found out. Except Newton would never go into elevators or telephone booths or closets. That was the only clue anyone had about him.

Arrival at Aunt Rose's was like at any of the aunt's houses. Pinching and kissing were first on the list of activities. Rose leaned down and put out a search warrant for Miriam's cheek under the huge straw brim. The only reason Miriam would wear the hat without a major tantrum was that it had strings that went under the chin to keep it on, with a little bead that went up and down like a cowboy hat. She could pretend she was Annie Oakley, or a cowhand on the range while everyone else thought she was a princess or a flower. Her aunt's two red lips would come at her, and squish against her skin, feeling like grapes when you press them. She touched her cheek and felt something sticky. The lips had left a huge red signature. Already her face would have to be washed, and she hadn't done anything.

Aunt Rose's house was a giant child-trap. First, there was the white carpet. Its color guaranteed that someone would spill red fruit punch on it. It was a sculpted rug with raised curlicues that invited people to stumble, and Aunt Rose said it was made of some new kind of material that breathed. "You probably have to mow it, eh, Rose?" Uncle Mort once asked. He would already have located the most comfortable easy chair in the room and was propped up in it like an inflated rubber raft. He always made a point to arrive early at Rose's so he could stake out the chair. The other easy chairs were actually disguised stones. They had cushions all right, but if you plunged down on one, your skeleton was rearranged on a permanent basis. Aunt Daisy claimed to have misplaced her sacroiliac one year when she sat on one of those chairs.

The center of attention in the living room was a large glass coffee table, shaped, Daisy told them, like a kidney. She and Uncle Mort had just put a kidney-shaped pool in their backyard. A penchant for organs ran through the family's circulatory system and included Uncle Mort gobbling up cow tongue and demanding it above all things for his birthday dinners, and it even filtered down to her brother Mike's collection of cat's eye marbles.

The glass table sat without a smudge – it had never known dust – a virgin glass table floating on the milky carpet, challenging anyone to touch it. The glass table had one object on it: a ceramic vase with a fragrant bouquet of plastic flowers. Aunt Rose put a sachet inside the vase scented with lily of the valley so people would think the flowers were real, as if fragrance were the ultimate proof that a flower had known the tug of the earth. When people sat on the couch the first thing they wanted to do was put something on the table like a purse or a foot. And the cousins wanted to play cards on it, and touch it with their fingers. Aunt Rose was convinced that children's hands secreted a sticky substance like flowers do nectar. Before you touch the Coke bottle, go and wash your hands. Before you wash your hands, go and wash your hands.

Like her sister Lily, Rose had no children. The family had suspected it was a mismatch with Newton from the beginning. After his disability involving small places, he was barely able to crawl to the dinner table, let alone think of touching Rose's body.

This one particular Sunday Miriam arrived with her mother and brother. Mike, reported to be a boy, never had to get as dressed up as Miriam. He had been allowed to wear his blue Cub Scout uniform; his crewcut had been wet down with Wild Root Creme Oil, which he insisted on using even though he had less hair than a drinking glass. He did have a little peak that stood straight up in front like a toothbrush when he used the oil. Their father never came with them to the Family Meetings. It had something to do with him not being Jewish. But he was friendly with Mort. They went fishing every year in Wisconsin, braving bears and wood shacks put together with good intentions alone with gaping holes that let in mosquitoes as big as fists. They didn't need an alarm clock the mosquitoes buzzed so loudly, Uncle Mort had once told her. Miriam never knew which stories to believe, so like everyone else she believed them all – even the one about the trout that two-stepped out of the lake and into the frying pan.

Mort was installed in his chair, and his daughter Julie, who was Miriam's age, was sitting *on* the glass coffee table, posing with her head thrown back. She was practicing to be a model like her mother, and there wasn't a moment you could catch her when her body wasn't flinging from one position to another. Aunt Daisy's clutch purse was reclining on the pristine table. Newton was wandering around the living room, saying, "Come in, come in" and patting children on the head. He looked as if he would have liked to swat Julie off the table, but he didn't know how. Aunt Rose was definitely not on patrol. Julie slid off the table when she saw Miriam. They immediately went over to the couch and began examining a whole new book of paper dolls Julie had brought with her. The dolls hadn't even been punched out yet. Miriam didn't mind her princess outfit any more – the paper dolls made up for it.

Daisy and Lily were in the kitchen putting cream cheese through a pastry tube and making it look like whipped cream, and Violet joined them. Mike located his two boy cousins, and they set off to the dining room to do nothing in particular but make noise, which is what boys spent most of their time doing when they weren't shooting marbles or telling girls to drop dead.

Mort was making feeble conversation with Newton in the living room. He completely ignored the girls because he didn't understand paper dolls, and he could think of nothing witty to say to them about flat cardboard figures dressed in underwear. "How's the job, Newt?" he asked.

"Pretty good," Newton said. "They took out the coffee machine, so now I bring a thermos." Newton had a small part-time job as a night watchman at a factory. It was easy enough to imagine how he guarded – he just had to walk around with a flashlight – but it was hard to imagine what he would have done if a prowler crossed his path. "Rose'll be down any minute," he said. "She spent the whole night cleaning. She likes the house to look nice for company – she was cleaning till dawn."

"We're not company," Mort said. "We're family." He raised his voice a little too loudly, and Daisy poked her head around the kitchen doorway to see what was causing her husband to yell.

Newton wandered around, lifting things up and putting them down. He was adrift at sea in his own living room. He needed the presence of Aunt Rose to anchor him to a chair where he could observe the changing of the tides without talking. He had never been the host before, and he was having trouble with the role.

"Do you have an ashtray?" Mort asked. From his pocket he pulled a giant cigar that was almost as tall as he was.

Newton looked around puzzled, searching under doilies and behind drapes, hoping to locate the desired object before Mort lit up. "I'm sure we have one," he said. When Mort struck the fatal blow, he started wringing his hands and walking in circles around the room scanning the tops of things for an ashtray that might have escaped his eye. "I can't remember where she keeps them."

Mort leaned over and carefully aimed, squinting his eye, and tossed the match stub through the air, making it land on the glass kidney. "Perfect hit!" he declared, producing a half inch ash with the puff of satisfaction he drew on the cigar.

Newton stared at the match as if it were a monster flea carrying the bubonic plague. If his wife didn't get down here soon her family was going to eat the rug and pick the plastic flowers. And the women in the kitchen. They sounded as if they were using every dish there, and tossing them down on the floor when they were finished. "Rose!" he screamed, "get down here." His bow tie came unclipped in his confusion, and he fumbled around on the carpet for it. Everyone came in to look at him. No one had ever heard Newton's voice above a low hum.

"What kind of monkeyshines are you up to?" Miriam's mother asked her from the kitchen doorway. At the time, Miriam was holding a paper girl by her waist and was far away in a castle being rescued by a prince. She and Julie looked at each other and shrugged.

When the women discovered why Newton was upset, they began to wonder about Aunt Rose too. "Miriam," her mother said in the voice that commanded her to sit up. "Go upstairs and tell Rose we're here." She turned to her sisters. "Maybe she fell asleep." Daisy raised an eyebrow. Aunt Rose never napped. She was afraid she would miss someone spilling something. "Go on, Miriam, tell her."

"Hurry up," Julie said, "I can't play all the parts myself."

Miriam reluctantly eased off the couch. She had managed to ditch her hat without anyone commenting on it. Men didn't have to keep their hats on inside, so why should she have to? Her mother wanted Aunt Rose to see it on, so she'd probably have to model it later. The stairs were covered with the white living room carpet, unlike the stairs at home where you could hear every hoofbeat. When she got to the top of the landing, she remembered the gloves. They were crumpled in her pocket.

Should she put them on? She reached for them. Aunt Rose always liked to see her and Julie wearing gloves like proper ladies, so she squeezed her fingers inside. They always made her feel like Mickey Mouse, not an elegant lady, because he wore white gloves too.

She tiptoed to the bedroom door. She had peeked in lots of times, but she had never actually put her foot over the threshold. It was dimly lit from the afternoon light, and there was no one to be seen. She stepped inside and immediately felt eyes staring at her, watching every move, wondering if the girl with the sticky fingers was going to take off her gloves and leave a sticky stain somewhere.

"Aunt Rose," Miriam whispered, "the family's here." No one answered her, so she tiptoed across the room, calling her aunt's name. There was a large four-poster bed. It looked like Aunt Rose's bed. It didn't look like Newton's bed at all. Maybe he slept under it. It was high enough off the floor so he could. "Aunt Rose," Miriam called, "the family's here." She traveled slowly across the room until she came to a door that was open a crack. It was Aunt Rose's private chamber – her dressing room. A feeling of dread came over her. No one was ever allowed in there, and what if her aunt came from somewhere else and saw her peeking? "Aunt Rose?" She let her voice lean into the room. A light was on. There was no answer, and very cautiously she pushed on the door a little. No one yelled, so she pushed it open a little more.

The chamber was revealed. Aunt Rose was asleep on a chair by a vanity. Miriam stared up open-mouthed. Hanging around the room were huge billowy corsets looking like dinosaur displays at the Natural History Museum. The hulking skeletons floated before her eyes, and for a moment she almost ran out. A lamp with a stiff shade like a skirt on a china doll was on. "Aunt Rose," she said, still not sure if she were going to be sent to jail for being in the room, "the family's here." She inched closer to her aunt, watching out for one of the corsets that might decide to swoop down on her at any second, and touched her aunt's bare arm. Her aunt was in a light blue nightgown. She didn't know that Aunt Rose had so much skin, because so much of it had never been let out at one time. She hugged her aunt as a greeting, and the hug was soft this time. Her cheek felt as if it were leaning into a feather pillow. Her aunt's huge breasts fell in waves under the gown, out of harness, on holiday. "Aunt Rose," Miriam said, "Uncle Newton wants you downstairs." She shook the sturdy arm with her white gloved hand, but the head leaning on the chest didn't move. Even though the picture was all right: the aunt asleep just after a bath, something in Miriam's brain registered *this is beyond me*. It was too quiet. When no one was talking, you could always hear Rose breathing – a kind of whistling came through her nose. "Aunt Rose?" she said again, leaving off the part about the family being there. "Mama!" she suddenly bellowed. She had a reputation for being the loudest screamer on the block. "Mama! Aunt Daisy! Mama!" Her body froze to the spot. She listened to the footsteps coming, into the room, past the bed, and barging into the chamber, forgetting that no one was allowed, not even the Flower Girls.

"Oh, my god," Lily said.

"Mama," Miriam cried, hugging her mother around the waist. "I tried to wake Aunt Rose, but she's asleep."

Shrieks followed. Everyone ran around at once yelling instructions, and Aunt Lily, tears on her face, began slapping Rose's cheeks in an effort to revive her. Miriam and Julie stood behind a dress form and watched their mothers and aunt cluster around the oldest Flower. Even Uncle Mort stood back. Newton finally came to the door. He had just made it up the stairs. His eyes bugged out and he looked to Mort for the answer. Uncle Mort took him out into the bedroom, and a terrible wailing noise ensued. "Rooooose, not Rooooose, Rooooose, not Rooooose," he chanted. Aunt Lily ran out to call on the telephone for help.

Mike and Julie's brothers came to the door, and Uncle Mort poked his cigar inside. "Stay out," Daisy said. "Only women allowed in here. You take Newton downstairs, and make him put his feet up – you know he has high blood pressure, and we don't want him to have another heart attack."

Mike stepped in and glared at the girls who were still huddled behind the dress form. "I said stay out," Daisy said, pointing her finger at Mike. When she didn't immediately chase her and Julie out too, Miriam knew she was safe, that even though she was a child, she was a woman too, which canceled out the child part. The door to the chamber was officially sealed after Lily slipped back in, saying an ambulance was coming. "Quick," Daisy said, "we have to get her presentable." Violet and Lily nodded in agreement. Her blue gown was lowered off her shoulders, revealing for the first time to so many eyes the enormous breasts that had hidden all these years in the whalebone caves. Freed from the gown they splayed out on either side. They were shot through with huge purple veins, like hoses, and pink nipples stretched as wide as the silver dollar Miriam got each year for her birthday. She stared, unable to look away. They weren't anything like her mother's breasts which were small and shy. Julie was looking too, standing crookedly on one foot, completely forgetting to pose like a model this time.

Violet stood behind propping Rose up at the shoulders, while Daisy and Lily each took an arm and fitted it through a brassiere strap. After shifting and shaking and leaning Rose forward a little, they managed to work the breasts into the brassiere, and Daisy and Lily held her from the front shoulders while Violet hooked her up in back. When they finished, the three sisters stood back admiring their work for a moment. "She would have died to have anyone see her uncorseted," Lily said. The irony of her comment reached her ears, and she buried her face in her hands. "I'm sorry, I didn't mean anything by that." She sobbed loudly and her sisters joined her, putting their arms around each other's shoulders.

"Mama," Miriam said. "Don't cry."

The three remaining Flower Girls whipped around. "You two shouldn't be in here," Daisy said. The invisible protection of being a woman had worn off.

"Is Aunt Rose alive?" Miriam asked.

The women exchanged looks. "She's in heaven now."

"But she's here in this room," Julie said.

"She's in the other place too, god rest her soul," Lily explained in a low voice. "You two better go downstairs and wait."

Outside the chamber they pushed past Mike and the other two boys. "We got to see," Miriam said.

"We could have too, if we had really wanted to," Mike said. His eyes roamed over the door, trying to see through it.

"No, you couldn't have. Only women were allowed in. Even Uncle Newton had to leave," she said, citing the ultimate proof, "and he was her husband." It was the first time in her life she had done something that her brother wasn't allowed to do. But the importance of that was overshadowed by what had happened to Aunt Rose. She thought she knew what had occurred, but she still was going to ask if they would ever see Aunt Rose again.

The ambulance driver confirmed that Aunt Rose was dead, and she was taken away. Uncle Mort followed in his car because he was the businessman and he knew about these things. He came back later to find everyone wandering around the house. Uncle Newton sat in the comfortable easy chair, his face in his hands, sobbing for hours. Mort paced around, angry that he didn't have a comfortable place to sit, and that he couldn't do anything about it. "Let's eat something," he said. "I'm starved."

The women looked shocked, but then Lily said that maybe food would make them all feel better. They didn't want to make it seem like a normal Family Meeting, so they put the food on the sideboard, and everyone came up and pecked at it from time to time. The fried chicken Aunt Daisy had made sat on a large platter. No one touched the white meat.

Uncle Newton followed Aunt Rose to the grave within the year. The Flower Girls all felt guilty about how they had never been too friendly to him, and had sometimes poked fun at his expense, so they made sure he had the coffin of a rich man, with brass swirls and silk lining. Naturally he wore his bow tie. But it must have been the final torture for him – all that splendor – because he didn't like to be in those small places.

The Koquettes

DARLENE IS A mole that lives in the back bedroom. She tunnels out on weekends to eat and go to the bathroom, and tunnels back to her room to sleep for incredible lengths of time during the day. Then she stays up to watch "Shock Theater" and the "Late Late Show" and whatever comes on after that. She is supposedly related to the Jerome family as sister and daughter, but birth records have been lost. She is fifteen years old and, to prove it, wears pancake make-up at all times.

Her orange face peers out of the crack in the door at Frank and Miriam. It says, "I'm not ready yet, so tell Mom to go fry an egg and quit her yapping." The door slams, and Frank says, "That's my sister Darlene – that was her longest appearance in months."

"Tell Darlene we're gonna eat soon," Mr. Jerome yells from down the hall.

Frank remains silent. "Okay," Miriam answers, even though she is only making a guest appearance in the Jerome household. The door opens again, and Darlene emerges in a blue terrycloth bathrobe missing most of the terry, and her face is lathered with Noxzema so only her eyes and lips show. She rushes past them, grumbling, and leaving a mentholated odor in her wake.

At dinner she is the last one to appear. Her empty chair is conspicuous as Frank's grandmother brings on the relish tray.

It becomes obvious that Miriam's aunts and mother are amateurs compared to this woman. At home radishes commonly turn into roses thanks to a little yellow rose-making machine, but here, everything is in disguise. The black olives are stuffed to look like penguins: cheddar cheese feet stand on cream cheese icebergs. The chopped liver has been sculpted into the shape of a life-size pineapple, with a real pineapple top for a hat. Deviled eggs stare up at them with pimento eyes. The cream cheese is in the form of a snowman: three balls atop one another with black olive coal pieces, an olive hat, and a shaved carrot muffler. Cauliflower pieces have been bent and snapped to look like daisies, and Ritz crackers are propped up in a snaky S shape designed to collapse like stacked dominoes when the first cracker is taken. An artist has been at work. She sits down at the table, smiling.

"Beautiful!" Mr. Jerome says, patting the hand of his mother-in-law.

Miriam is too stunned to say anything.

"Eat!" Mr. Jerome continues, gesturing to her.

There is no way that she is going to lead the destruction of all the tidbits or be known as the One Who Pulled the First Cracker. She steps on Frank's foot under the table. It must be connected by wire to his arm because he reaches out for a deviled egg.

Just then a perfumy smell enters the room followed by a pair of heavy black eyelashes under which Darlene can be found.

"She was in the bathroom growing all that fur on her eyes," Mr. Jerome says.

Everyone chuckles except Darlene. She glares sullenly at her father and sits down at the table.

"I'm glad you woke up, it's your parents' anniversary," the grandmother says, putting a dab of cream cheese and a mutilated cauliflower piece on Darlene's plate.

"I'm not hungry," she says. "I'm not gonna eat."

"Why don't you wait in your room then, until we open the presents?" Mr. Jerome says.

"Now dear," Monica says – Frank's mother has told Miriam to call her by her first name – "we do have company. Let her sit at the table." She tosses her tawny, beauty parlor extravaganza flip from one shoulder to the other.

That settles it. Mr. Jerome decides to change the subject and talk tactfully about his business partner's teenage daughter who is a model daughter and knows how to dress and behave and have dates and doesn't play loud music at three A.M. "God knows," he says to Monica and anyone in earshot, "if I had known I was going to raise a nocturnal animal, I would have thought twice about having kids."

A slight rift appears to exist between father and daughter. "So," Miriam says, "what grade are you in?"

"We don't have grades in high school – we have years." Darlene glares at her, but there is a curious look that follows.

"You and Frank go together?"

"Yes, that is, we date."

The rest of the dinner is brought in by the grandmother slave. Chicken soup, unsculpted dried out roast beef and noodle pudding.

Everyone digs in pretending hunger, except Darlene. When Miriam has a large piece of roast beef in her mouth, Darlene asks, "Do you and Frank sleep together?"

"That's enough!" Mr. Jerome roars. A fist bangs on the table. Monica looks on calmly, mostly at Miriam. Maybe she expects the question to be answered. Yes, Monica, I sleep with him. We're so crazy about each other's bodies that he attacked me in the den right under your noses not a half hour ago.

"Get to your room," Mr. Jerome says to his daughter.

"It's okay, really," Miriam says, even though it is not okay that a snotty fifteen-year-old has asked her that.

"You shut up," he tells her.

"Dad," Frank yells, "you're shouting at my girlfriend. We can leave, you know."

The shouting stops because the most dreaded threat has been made: it is hard enough to get Frank to come home once in a while, and they are not about to chase him away. Mr. Jerome gestures once more and Darlene slumps away from the table.

When she is sheltered by the hall, they hear huge sobs coming from her and then her bedroom door slams.

"Pay no attention," Mr. Jerome says, "She thinks she's some kind of big cheese around here, trying to push us around."

"I guess all fifteen-year-olds are the same," Miriam says.

When she was fifteen she skulked around the house too, only she was lucky. Mr. Jerome wasn't there. She was always compared to her cousin Julie, who was the same age as Miriam, but more brilliant, beautiful, well-mannered, artistic, poised, and athletic than Miriam. Both girls were thin, but Miriam was thinner where Julie was fatter, and shorter where Julie was taller. Neither body should have ever shared a piece of clothing, but Miriam was blessed with Julie's worn out dresses.

Julie, in her clothes that fit, had dates with flesh and blood boys who obviously liked her for the wonderful things she wore. "Nonsense," her mother said, "her clothes have nothing to do with it – she's just a popular girl, that's all."

Her life changed briefly when two girls from school asked her to join their club. Miriam was elected to have the party for the coming month. Her mother was not prepared for what walked in the front door. "Little zombies," she called them later. Every girl wore a wool jacket with the name Koquettes scripted on the back. The boys who came were from the Avengers and they wore wool jackets too. To say that the dancing was cheek to cheek does not give credit to the other body parts which made contact that night. At some point a girl ran out on the porch and yelled into the night – more specifically to Dr. and Mrs. Farmington across the street: "I want to get laid!" This made Miriam's membership in the club a short one. Miriam went back to writing wistful poetry, and buying powders and lotions to cover up her olive skin, and daydreaming that the leader of the Avengers would kidnap her and take her to his lair.

*

It is now after dinner at the Jeromes'. They are still at the table because the anniversary presents have to be opened, and there is a tradition in the family that only allows people to sit on the soft couches and chairs in the living room before dinner. After dinner you stay at the table and *schmooze*, her Aunt Daisy's favorite activity.

"Daisy and I went to high school together," Monica says, answering a question. "Now we're in the same hospital club." It was through these latter-day Koquettes' machinations that Miriam and Frank met – that is, were fixed up.

Must women belong to clubs their whole lives? Miriam does not want to talk about the dread diseases Monica and Daisy raise money for, so she blatantly changes the subject. "Are there any elk in Elk Grove Village?" she asks.

For a moment Mr. Jerome frowns. The red light on his computer flashes "does not compute" but then he smiles. "Oh, yes," he says, "there's a whole grove of them as you drive off the expressway – Sonny Boy will show them to you."

"I had a dream about elk once," Miriam continues, hoping to keep this alive and diseases dead. Everyone looks at her with expectation. "Well, in my dream there was a whole herd of elk behind a fence and I had to gather them together to take them back to the YMCA. So I led them into a big truck, like a bread truck, and somehow got them all into a brown paper sack."

"And then what happened?" Mr. Jerome inquires.

"Nothing. That was it. I woke up."

They are sitting in stunned silence, staring at her. Sonny Boy has taken up with a deranged person.

"That's a nudnik dream," Mr. Jerome says.

"Don't you mean Young Men's *Hebrew* Association?" Monica asks. "Why would you have a Christian association in your dream?"

"I wanna see my presents," Mr. Jerome says.

"*Our* presents, dear – remember it's our anniversary, not your birthday." Monica smiles. "Our thirty-first anniversary," she tells Miriam.

The grandmother is sent to get the cake, and Frank is ordered to locate and deliver Darlene. When his face protests, Miriam says, "I'll get her." Everyone looks at her with expressions that say how can you do what we can't, but no one tries to stop her. People in this house recognize favors when they are being done.

There is no answer when she knocks on the bedroom door. She says finally, "It's Miriam – open up." Minutes go by. "I'm alone . . ." After a long while there is the sound of a door being unbolted. Darlene's room is an apartment in a dangerous neighborhood. "What you want?" she mumbles, showing a resentful eye through the crack. Her make-up is streaked and muddy from mascara. Miriam tells her about the presents and the cake.

"Wanna come in?" Darlene asks.

In this surprising change of events, Miriam manages to find a "sure" in her repertoire of quick answers, and the door opens enough for her to squeeze inside Darlene's bedroom. Make-up bottles and hair curlers grow like mushrooms on every flat surface of the room. Hanging on the wall are posters of the Beatles and Simon and Garfunkle. There are clothes everywhere, balled, wadded, and spread-eagled on chairs, the bed and the floor. When Miriam thinks twice about sitting on the bed filled with squashed up underwear, Darlene says, "Don't worry, it's all clean stuff, I just don't put my things away. It drives my mother wild." She smiles, and Miriam smiles back at her.

"So you're Frankie's new girl. You look awful young; he's kind of old you know."

"I'm twenty-three," Miriam says. "And for your information, your brother isn't old. Twenty-eight is not old."

"So you can still wear knee socks when you're twenty-three. That's a relief. I thought you had to dress like Mom."

"Sure. Jeans even."

This is a big hit with Darlene. She pulls out her scrapbook which has every fact about the Beatles ever brought to light. Then Miriam helps her comb through the rat's nest she's gotten her hair into. They take off the smeared make-up with one of the many creams that are around. There is actually skin beneath the orange, smooth white skin that is unblemished. Not even the hint of a pimple as a possible explanation of why she frosts her face like a cake. The skin squints because it hasn't seen incandescent or sun light in months. "If I had beautiful skin like yours," she tells Darlene, "I'd never put a drop of anything on it. I don't even have beautiful skin. Mine is just the right shade to turn purple in fluorescent lighting. And I don't use make-up."

Darlene stares at her like she is talking a rare dialect of Polish. "Not use make-up," she says. "Wow. I even wear make-up in the shower in case there's a fire and we have to evacuate."

Miriam manages to convince her to wear only one layer of plain powder, and to remove the gigantic eyelashes because she says, "They make you look like Minnie Mouse."

*

"My child!" Mr. Jerome shouts when they come to the table. "Where did you find her?"

When Darlene blushes her face turns red now. She is still grumpy, but takes a piece of cake from her grandmother. Miriam is treated like a homecoming queen. Her square of cake has a big red rose on it, created by the pastry tubes of the grandmother.

Mr. Jerome and Monica, satisfied their daughter has returned to the land of the living, remember it's their anniversary. Mogen David wine appears on the table, and toasts are made to the sanctity of marriage. Each time a toast is made, everyone must click the glass of everyone else. The grandmother brings the presents over and Monica opens one with her name on it. It is good for a gasp of pleasure and a lewd giggle. "Let's see," Frank says.

"It's too embarrassing. . . ." But one second later she extracts a black silky something from the box. She holds it up to her body. Supposedly it is a nightgown, but where the breasts fit are lacy apertures. Mr. Jerome leans back in his chair for a better look. "Go model it for us," he says.

"Da-dee," Darlene says, shaking her head, trying to silence him.

Frank remembers the philodendron he's brought, and rushes to the car to retrieve it. Monica ooo's and ah's over it, saying it's exactly what she wanted.

"I'm surprised it hasn't frozen its *schlong* off," Mr. Jerome says.

"Daddy!" Darlene screams. She glares at him, determined to stop him.

"Don't worry," Miriam says, "the plant can't speak Yiddish – the owner of the store where we got it is Greek."

Everyone laughs except Darlene. Suddenly she smiles, and then laughs. "That was funny," she says.

There is no question about it. This homecoming queen will reign forever. The looks that Mr. Jerome and Monica are sending in Miriam's direction are looks of love. She can rest easy now. There is no way Monica is going to put her down the sink disposal, as Frank has said she did to his previous girlfriend.

"Why don't you stay over?" Mr. Jerome says. "We have plenty of room."

"What a wonderful idea," Monica says. Her words are oozing out through a pastry tube. "It's such a long drive back to the city."

By the time she and Frank are putting on their coats, Mr. Jerome and Monica have practically invited her to move in rent free. Frank they haven't mentioned as much. He can come to visit often, but Miriam can live there in the Jerome palace. She will make Darlene a wonderful sister.

She hugs Darlene good-bye and gets the grateful permission from the parents to have her over some Saturday. She is smothered in x's and o's from Mr. Jerome and Monica. In a short evening she has eaten a cheddar cheese penguin foot, changed a mole into a person, told her elk in a paper bag dream, and managed not to call Monica by first name or last. Unfortunately no awards exist for the Most Bizarre Activity at a Dinner Party.

"You hang onto this gem," Mr. Jerome tells Frank.

*

They are in the car at last, heading back to her tiny apartment in Old Town.

"My little social worker," Frank says, reaching for her cheek in a pinch.

"Hush up," she answers, putting her hand on his leg. She tries to blank out the scared face of Darlene peering at her through the door of the bedroom. Every time she sees the face, she relives the most pleasant moments of her teenage years: hiding out in her bedroom . . . so anyone who wondered would think she had gone out of town, and not know that she didn't have a date. She didn't even know enough to scrunch up her clothes to aggravate her mother, as Darlene has learned to do.

"My sister only takes her meals in her room – you don't know what it meant to see her at the table." Frank glances over to her.

"I do grandmothers too," Miriam says. "As a hobby. When I leave that publishing company every day, I go on a grandmother hunt. Just wait till we go back next time – your grandmother will never make another pineapple chopped liver – she will vomit at the sight of one, I promise."

Frank Jerome laughs, and picks up her hand, kissing the palm. "Let's get this football helmet home."

The VW, which Miriam thinks of as a tin mushroom, revs up and passes a Jewel T truck in order to make the exit at Ontario.

Florida

Hawaiian Dukes

*For Lee Sanders, in memoriam,
and for John King.*

SIMON WAS A man who wore brightly colored shirts. One of the shirts was red with white lotus blossoms. Another was yellow with red dragons. One had shapes of the islands of Hawaii printed on the material. He wore a different one every day, and they all reminded him of his boyhood on Ewa Beach near Waikiki.

He had started gathering his shirts when they first appeared on the racks at J. C. Penney and later K-Mart. At first there were just a few, but in time it became a craze, and Simon noticed people wearing these shirts everywhere. He now lived in Florida, near the Gulf of Mexico, where the breezes blew gently and sashayed through the palm fronds, bringing him back to his childhood. He often drove by the Vinoy Basin in St. Petersburg hoping to glimpse tourists in their splashy shirts meandering along side the palm trees with Tampa Bay glistening in the distance.

He had gone to J. C. Penney to check on the uniforms for his high school band. His wife, Elena, was with him, and he was listening to the thwacking sound her flip flops made as she walked next to him.

He spotted the first Hawaiian shirt on the end of a rack of polo shirts. It was blue with white pineapples stamped on it. And it was large. It would fit Simon's ballooning girth.

"What's this?" Simon asked, veering to the left, leaving Elena in the aisle.

"Gau-dee," Elena said.

"Yeah. I kind of like it." Simon carried the shirt on its hanger over his shoulder to the dressing room. It felt so good, this cool, colorful cotton with pineapples dancing all over his torso. The sparkling sands of Hawaii were winking at him as he turned in front of the mirror. He liked the way his white undershirt formed a triangle at the neckline – just as his father had looked so long ago when he changed from his bleached white navy uniform with golden braid. There was a pineapple right on the pen pocket of this shirt, and Simon patted it before taking one more glance in the mirror.

"I don't think so," Elena said, when he leaned out of the dressing room.

"Wrap it up," Simon told the clerk a minute later.

The young man folded over the stiff material. "This is only cotton. We're getting in some rayon ones next week."

"I'll stay with cotton." He took the bag. What was the clerk trying to do? Had he thought Simon was sucker enough to buy some cheap shirts that would fall apart in the first washing?

After a time, he had the grandest collection of Hawaiian shirts in all of St. Petersburg. His friends came from far and wide for a viewing – there were at least one hundred shirts hanging like a misplaced flower garden in his closet. People sat on the edge of the bed and waited. Simon opened the closet slowly.

"Amazing," his friends said. "Who would believe this?" they asked. Only Elena was miffed. The shirts were quickly devouring her side of the closet, until she moved all of her clothes to the guest closet and threatened to put a lock on it if a colored thread or hibiscus flower bloomed among her pale silk shirts and tweedy skirts. In time, though, she came to enjoy the exhibits, and softly smiled as he burbled on about this or that shirt.

*

One day Simon found himself in a Checker taxi with an armload of band uniform hats. He had to rush the hats back to school for a rehearsal of an all-Sousa retrospective.

"Step on it," he told the driver. He reached into his pocket for a handkerchief and dabbed his forehead. It was a scorcher out.

"Step on it?" the driver asked. "Man, you gotta be kidding. Nobody says that to a cabbie. We gotta obey the rules as much as civilians."

Simon was annoyed but didn't say anything. He stared at the back of the driver, hoping his x-ray vision would sear him. Wait a minute. His back was filled with frangipani flowers, tendrils winding over and under the blossoms. The driver was wearing a Hawaiian shirt. Simon's shirt was brighter, a lemon yellow with Hawaiian beauties dancing the hula in grass skirts and leis. It was his favorite one.

"Nice shirt," Simon mumbled. "Myself, I collect them."

He thought he heard the driver snort at him, but it could have been the air conditioner kicking up.

"That'll be $5.40," the driver said, folding down the meter bar. Then he opened his door and got out of the cab.

As Simon pulled out the box of band uniform hats, he noticed the driver was an extra large to his large. The buttons were doing a tug of war over his belly. The man looked to be his father's age, and the shirt . . . spare the eyes. The shirt was black, not blue as Simon had thought in the cab, and it was made of that shiny, slinky material that Simon knew was cheap. The guy was a real loser, a first class chump.

"Thanks, pal," the driver said when Simon handed him the money. He rubbed his hand over his mouth for a second. "I can't help noticing your hula shirt," he said.

"Yours is . . . quite nice too," Simon answered, feeling generous. The old guy needed a boost.

"Well, now, dude," the driver said. "I didn't exactly say your shirt was nice."

Simon smiled. "What's that?"

"Man, your shirt is the pits."

Simon felt his face turning red. The bright sunlight was causing him to squint at the driver. "I don't see any need for insults. I have a whole closet full of shirts that would take you down a few buttons."

"Don't count on it, man. You mean to say you collect those

things? That shirt you're wearing, man, let me be the first –
that shirt is below garbage."

"Your shirt is black," Simon hissed. "No one wears a black
Hawaiian shirt. And it's made of that cheap material, that rayon."

"Man, what you don't know." The driver shook his head and
smiled at Simon. "Allow me to introduce myself – I'm Chaz the
Checker man, and someone's been feeding you a line of bull."

Simon leaned against the cab, knowing he had to get inside
the high school, but he was unable to move. He squinted at Chaz.
"What the hell are you talking about?"

"The dude wants to know what I'm talking about. Your shirt,
that's what I'm talking about. Your shirt is a Penney's special."
He swiped at his mouth again and shook his head. "I'm gonna
tell you this, give you my trade secrets, man, because I'm positive
you won't understand, and you'll go on buying your so-called
Hawaiian shirts. But people like you – damn, you make me so
mad. It's like you go to the five and ten and get a gen-u-ine repro
of a Rembrandt and hang it over your couch because it matches
the color and you think it looks nice. That's what your shirt is."

Simon tried to say something, but Chaz held up his hand. "Now
this is a shirt." He tugged at the hem of the material. "This is
a Duke. You know, a Duke Kahanamoku. Circa 1945. Matching
pocket. With collar points that go on forever. Coconut buttons
and double stitching. Black background, which makes it rare.
And made of the best rayon. Feels like you're making love when
it's next to your skin."

"What's a matching pocket?" Simon mumbled.

"You wouldn't know one if it bit you. Look at how the flower
on the pocket perfectly meets up with the stem on the material.
You can hardly tell it's a pocket the design is so perfect."

"Big deal. The whole shirt is made of rayon – quite inferior to
cotton."

Chaz smiled. "Maybe you didn't hear me right, dude. I said
this shirt was from '45. That means it's been knocking and bop-
ping around all these long years. This is made of rayon manufac-
tured before the fire."

"What fire?" Simon asked.

"Man. The fire that destroyed a rayon factory and burned up the old rayon formula along with it. 1952. They never were able to duplicate the formula. So old rayon shirts, they bring in a pretty penny." He jingled some coins in his pocket for effect.

Simon ran his fingers through his curly hair. "I don't know what to say. If these shirts are so special, how do you even find them?"

"Junk stores – that's the best place. The fancy places that steam the wrinkles out of the old clothes and call them vintage – they want too much. Naw, you gotta go to the junk stores, and Florida is a gold mine. All the dudes from W-W-2 who retired down here brought vans full of shirts. They move into smaller houses and condos and there's no room for the shirts. Their old ladies start screaming about closet space so they pack the shirts off to the Goodwill. That's where I come in."

"How do you know all this?"

"I'm one of those vet dudes – yeah, I was there – in the Islands, W-W-2, only I kept my shirts." He held out his hand. "Gotta hit the streets, man. Living to be made. Keep cool. And remember: *Shaheen, Lauhala, Duke Kahanamoku/ Shaheen, Lauhala, Duke Kahanamoku.*

"What does it mean?" Simon called after him.

Chaz rolled down the window of his cab. "Labels, man. Labels. Look for the labels. If a shirt doesn't have a label, it's only half a shirt. Now, *ua mau ke ea oka aina ika pono* and I'm outta here."

*

Simon sat in front of his closet staring at his hundred plus shirts. He tried to be proud of them, but now he wasn't so sure. When he explained to Elena that Penney's shirts and single stitching in the Hawaiian shirt world didn't make it anymore, she asked him to speak English.

"What I mean is, I want to try to find some of those other kinds of shirts. The kind this guy Chaz told me about."

"I think you have sunstroke," Elena said. "You are not spending more money on a whole other collection of shirts. Where would you put them, for one thing?" She eyed her closet door. "Oh, no."

Simon realized there was truth in her reasoning. And what if these other shirts didn't exist in the quantity that this Chaz said they did? He'd have to go looking for himself.

*

He sat in the trusty Valiant that he and Elena had driven down to Florida five years before. He could see through the display windows that the Kidney Foundation Thrift Store was crawling with people.

Inside he breathed the stale air. They didn't even have air conditioning, just the world's largest fan at one end of the store creating a gale as Simon walked toward the racks of men's shirts. He began to notice that people had shopping carts. They couldn't hold enough of the rags in their arms. They had to pile them in a cart. One woman, who was dressed in an all-white garment like a choir robe, had her basket filled with items that were pure white – no colors at all. Further along a man was talking to a rack of hats – those kinds of hats his mother used to wear with feathers and a veil.

In Men's Shirts he noticed the worst thing possible: a man was speeding along, his cart piled with Hawaiian shirts. Simon panicked. He was going to get every single one, and there wouldn't be any left for Simon. He felt dismal. The man was obviously a collector and had beaten him to it. Simon walked slowly along the rack, poking at shirts. He saw a Hawaiian one and tugged it out. J. C. Penney label. He went further down, keeping one eye on the collector. Something sleazy hit his fingers. He eased the shirt from the rack. A black short sleeve with green and orange foliage, kind of abstract. The material wiggled back and forth in the breeze, and then Simon remembered. His mother had taken him as a boy to a Waikiki nightclub. And there Arthur Godfrey was, playing his ukulele, wearing a shirt that drifted in the breeze off the ocean like this shirt was drifting. This was A SHIRT. Simon was sure of it. He looked at the label. La la . . . Lauhala. Lauhala. That was it. That was one of them. *Shaheen, Lauhala, Duke Kahanamoku/Shaheen, Lauhala, Duke Kahanamoku.* And it was a LARGE. The guy ahead of him didn't have a clue. Simon felt faint in the heat and excitement of finding a keeper. He rushed to the check-out, paid his dollar and a quarter and jumped in his car, keeping the shirt in the bag, wanting to savor it when he got home.

*

He had a plan now that involved Hocus Pocus, the annual anti-nuke gathering in the park. Simon and Elena always went as spectators, but this year would be different. Simon strung a clothesline between two trees and became an entrepreneur. His entire collection of Penney shirts dangled in front of him. By noon he had sold half of his collection at five dollars a crack. People were grabbing at them faster than he could make change. He watched the arms of a bulky man loop into the hula dancer shirt, and was surprised that his once favorite looked so flat and ugly to him now. Now that he had a Lauhala.

The park emptied out around five o'clock. Simon unknotted the bare clothesline. He had cash flow and a closet waiting like a cave for shirts to hibernate. What more opportunity could he want? He would hunt down the shirts and fill his closet with the real objets d'art.

"Hey, dude, I saw your scam here today." It was Chaz, sneaking up behind him. Naturally he had on a fancy shirt, dark blue with medallions and tiny flower shapes in regular rows, a border design, Simon had learned from reading a book about decorative shirts.

"So is that a Kala Ka-ua or a Pali or a Ho Aloha?" Simon asked.

"Whoa. The Penney's expert has gotten himself some education. I'm impressed. This, my man, is a Duke Kahanamoku. The cream of Hawaiian shirts."

Simon snapped the legs closed on a folding table.

"I'll have to get me a few, then."

"Maybe you can. Maybe you *can* find some Dukes. They're hard to come by. But of course, you'll never get your palms on THE SHIRT."

Simon's eyebrows flicked upward. "What do you mean, THE SHIRT?"

"THE Duke, my man. Every serious collector knows about the Duke, dreams about it. I've been after it for years."

"Tell me about it."

"No such luck. All I'll say is if you look from here to eternity, a ringer like you won't find it. I am going down to the Pier next Saturday to meet a woman, you know, a gypsy dealer – she drives around the state, and she just might know something."

"Know about what?"

"THE Shirt, man. The Duke. If you want to slide on by, you can watch the master at work."

*

Simon was thoroughly confused. At home he sat in the dark, chanting "*Shaheen, Lauhala, Duke Kahanamoku/Shaheen, Lauhala, Duke Kahanamoku*" until his ears buzzed and his eyes glazed over. Finally it hit him. "If you look from here to eternity . . . " the words came back to him. From *Here To Eternity!* That was it. The movie with Montgomery Clift. In a frenzy he went out to rent it, driving in a storm so fierce the palm trees bent over the roads. He was always amazed how elastic their trunks were.

He watched the black and white movie, and IT was revealed to him: Montgomery Clift in his death scene wearing a Hawaiian shirt with palms. Through the palms is Diamond Head, and the palms span the shirt, as big as small trees.

Simon was in a fever. From film books he learned that the original shirt had a blue background. After school every day he made his rounds, looking for THE Shirt. Salvation Army, Goodwill, League of Mercy, Kidney Foundation, John 3:16. He hit them all, skimming through the racks, expert at touch, at finding the limp and silky feel in his fingers. He made an unusual haul during the week. Several monsters, as he now thought of them instead of keepers, came his way, and by the end of the week he had six of them in his closet. All had cost under three dollars apiece, and each was in top condition. The feel of old rayon had gotten into his bones, and they ached for more. They ached for THE Shirt specifically.

Saturday he drove down to the Pier. Chaz hadn't told him where or when, so he went early and cruised around the pyramid-shaped building. Maybe he could get to the woman first, before Chaz showed. Only the fishermen were there, and a few pelican fellows hoping for a handout, flapping their wings, causing the fishermen to shoo them away. He parked his car by the Vinoy Basin and waited. After a long while a VW van drove by, old and green and familiar. Simon had had one back in the early seventies. No heater and rust in the floorboard – he didn't see how any of them could still exist, and yet here was this survivor. The van stopped a few feet in front of his car.

Simon got out. A woman appeared from the driver's side, around thirty-five years old, wearing shorts and a tank top, no bra, pretty curves, silver earrings moving like wind chimes, fuzzy blond hair on her legs. Simon took this all in with one gulp. "Great van you have there," he said, smiling at her. "I used to . . ."

The woman rolled her eyes at him.

"That is, I collect Hawaiian shirts, and I've heard that you might have a certain Duke Kahan . . . Duke – the Montgomery Clift Duke that is . . ." This wasn't going well. The woman was looking at him with an amused smile.

"Yeah, Chaz told me all about you. Sure, I got the Duke in my van here."

Simon felt like jumping in the air and snapping his heels together. Instead he calmly cleared his throat. "I'd be interested in making an offer on it." He glanced down 2nd Avenue leading to the Pier. Chaz was nowhere in sight.

The woman looked around too. "So make an offer if you're going to. I have to get on the road."

How much should he offer her? He usually paid under five dollars for the monsters he found. "Fifty dollars. I'll give you fifty dollars." That should obliterate any offer Chaz would make. Simon reached into his pocket, hoping his wallet held that much.

"Fifty dollars. Wow. That's going to be hard for me to turn down."

"Of course, I have to see the shirt first."

"Sure. I've got it right here." She slid open the side door, and before Simon could peek in, Chaz climbed out, and HE WAS WEARING THE SHIRT. He held his arms up triumphantly like a boxer, and did a complete three-sixty so Simon could admire it. There it was, brilliant blue in the sunlight with the palms swaying on the material in the breeze from Tampa Bay, and through the palms was Diamond Head, pink and iridescent, more beautiful than Simon had imagined.

He reached out to touch a sleeve, but Chaz swooped back. "Don't you know the rules of the museum? Look but don't touch. Right, sweet stuff?"

The woman smiled.

"But we had a deal," Simon yelled.

"Hey, my man. What's this talk now? I go and tell you about this, just so you could come here and be in the presence of the Duke of Dukes, and what do you try to do? You try to ace me out, man. I don't think I like that."

Simon looked to the woman for help. She circled her arm through Chaz's and looked over at a sailboat in the Basin.

"Besides," Chaz said. "Your fifty dollars wouldn't touch it. I paid ten times that. This is the only mint copy in blue in the whole state. I'm sure of it."

"You paid five hundred dollars for that shirt?" Simon felt a major part of his skeleton collapse inside. That was how much he had gotten for his one hundred shirts. What had he gotten involved in? Before the woman closed the van, he glimpsed what looked to be hundreds of shirts hanging neatly on racks. Every one of them a monster no doubt. And the biggest monster of them all was floating on that bastard's gut.

As he got into the Valiant, Chaz came over and said, "*Ua mau ke ea oka aina ika pono.*"

"What the hell does that mean?"

"'Life of the land is preserved in righteousness.' It's right on the Duke label in this very shirt. But you'll never see it. I won't let you get that close. You're dealing with a master here."

Simon cranked up his window and drove away.

Months went by. Simon made his rounds every day after school. He bagged a number of monsters, built up his collection, and was even modestly proud of it. He had to admit, these shirts looked a whole lot better than his original collection. Elena even took to wearing some of them, and she hung the ones she wore in her own closet.

Then one day a new student named Rita who played French horn in his band came up and asked him, "You like those flowered shirts, don't ya?"

"Why do you ask?"

"My mother said to mention it. I have an uncle who just died. He had a whole bunch of shirts he brought back from Hawaii. You know, from during the war. My mother said he never even wore them. They're still in cellophane."

"Really?" Simon asked. "I don't suppose they're for sale?"

"My mother says you can *have* them. You can come by his house tomorrow. All our relatives are coming in, so it'll be kind of crowded."

Tomorrow. Relatives. Crowded. Someone who's a collector was bound . . . "Tell your mother, that is, ask your mother if she would be so kind as to put the shirts . . . away from the . . . that is away for me. With all those people they might get lost. Tell her to hide . . . put them in the washing machine or someplace like that."

"All right."

"Promise you'll tell her?"

"Sure."

*

On his rounds that evening Simon kept patting his shirt pocket, feeling the crinkle of the paper with the address the girl had given him. He would go there tomorrow and he would reel in the biggest catch of all. The Duke would be there, he was sure of it. And other monsters in mint condition.

That night he dreamt that when the relatives arrived, one of them turned on the washing machine and all the colors ran together in the shirts. And later in the dream it was the oven. The stupid woman had put them in the oven, and someone turned it on. When he woke, he was convinced that the girl was a plant in his class – she was new this semester. She must be Chaz's relative, and this whole thing was a hoax. He decided not to go, but when he got into his car that afternoon, he headed away from home, toward Snell Isle. It wasn't shirts, he realized, but the possibility of them, that pulled him through the streets sizzling with a rain that wasn't going to stop any time soon.

Fauna in Florida

THERE'S NOTHING BETWEEN you and an alligator except a lot of humid air and a whole lot of bad wishes from both of you.

*

Gotta watch out that alligator   watch out   watch out.

*

Feeding time's at 5 P.M. at Sawgrass Lake. The cars on I-275 that skate along one side of the park form a background hum like piped-in restaurant music that you can never get away from. The alligators slither along the bank of the skinny lake which looks like a stream and some of them swim on over to the bridge where the ranger throws things like chickens and skinned animals that are probably rabbits into the water and the jaws scissor open and grab the animal which is already dead meat. Then the alligators dive below, drowning their meal just as if it's alive and kicking.

*

Gotta watch out that alligator   watch out   watch out.

*

Everyone wants to see the 'gators. Some of them go to Busch Gardens and stand behind fences and glass gawking at the slithery boggy-looking reptiles. Every year some kid falls into the pit somewhere.

*

Gotta watch out that alligator   watch out   watch out.

*

You're not really a part of Florida till you've seen a 'gator in the wild. A woman laments she's been in St. Pete twelve years and never saw one yet. All you have to do is sit by a lake and observe. Not any special alligator-infested lake. Just a fresh water lake, a pond really. You know the kind – the ones that are dug out to make an apartment complex look pretty or to make a housing development more appealing. If you wait long enough, you'll see a 'gator. That 'gator might be coming or going. Those things migrate all over the city, and there aren't any fences to keep them in. That's what seeing a 'gator in the wild is: seeing it over by Mirror Lake one block from city hall. Some people in the apartments take fistfuls of marshmallows and call out, "Here, alligator," and throw the marshmallows into the water and wait for the smack as the jaws open and close. Sometimes they even name the alligators. Sammy. Josie. Alexander.

*

Gotta watch out that alligator   watch out   watch out.

*

A woman living out on 4th Street got up one morning and stuck her bent up toes into her terrycloth scuffies by feel – the morning light didn't get to her bedroom because of the huge bougainvillea bush with its killer thorns she had by her window to keep out intruders. She tied her terry bathrobe and scuffed along the hall into the bathroom. No, you guessed wrong. No alligator had worked its way up the toilet pipe. None was floating in the bathtub covered with bubbles. She eventually made her way to the front door to get her newspaper. She opened the door and bent down and reached out her arm by habit and almost lost her wedding ring and the charm bracelet she never took off that had ten golden heads attached by gold loops, one head for each grandkid. Their birthdays were stamped on the heads. The girls had ponytails and the boys had crewcuts. She almost lost these things because there was what looked to her like a real-life gray-green four-footed slimy-mouthed alligator waiting for a meal. His two front feet were on the plastic wrapper of the paper. Well, the woman got her door closed, and a special detachment of the local police arrived. The Alligator Relocation Squad moved right into the neighborhood with giant nets and ropes and stun guns. If you can keep the tail from wagging and the mouth tied shut, you're pretty much home free is how they look at it. After they got the 'gator all trussed up, they stood around with Polaroids and took each other's pictures, and of course the paper came and did a little feature on it in the city section. Then they put it in their relocation vehicle, which looked suspiciously like a paddy wagon, and they took it across town, making sure it was still a little stunned. Then they untied it and left it on the edge of some pond in a neighborhood very much like the woman's on 4th street.

*

Gotta watch out that alligator   watch out   watch out.

*

One theory goes that there's only a certain number of alligators in St. Petersburg, and they get antsy, and spend their time migrating from lake to lake, pond to pond. Some of the most popular watering holes are Lake Maggiore, Mirror Lake, Crescent Lake, and the lake at Eckerd College which probably has a name but no one uses it. But there are hundreds of others and they all are safe harbors for reptiles. You can't even trust a rain puddle, some people say. Sure, some 'gators reproduce, but they're not what you would call prolific. They don't have the same energy as rabbits or mosquitoes.

*

What will you do to see an alligator? What will you sacrifice? One artist did it this way. She was looking for a whole slew of alligators to paint. She went to Busch Gardens. Wasn't good enough for her. There was the matter of a fence keeping her back, keeping her from getting close in where she could see detail, as she put it. She spent weeks going to different enclosures, but always the 'gators were too far away. She had seen plenty in the wild over the years, and knew it wouldn't be good to get too close, because then she'd want to run instead of paint. But she had to get her 'gators. She had been painting fish, and it was time to move on to alligators. Pretty soon, it was all she could think of. She had dreams about alligators rooting around her closets and soaping up in the shower.

She talked about alligator-watching parties. A friend gave her binoculars, but it wasn't the same. She discovered that people didn't want to talk alligators. They were too busy dealing with other fauna, rounding up palmetto bugs and running from wolf spiders. "Everyday terrors," someone told her. Finally, one night she was watching TV, trying to take her mind off of alligators, when what should come on but an ad for an alligator farm, a place that grew alligators like corn, and harvested them for fancy restaurants to put them on the menu under the label of "Delicacies." Next day she called them and figured the direct approach was the best, so she told them she was an artist and just had to see their alligators.

"We got postcards," the man on the phone said.

Well, it was clear he didn't understand, but he told her to come on ahead, that feeding time was around two P.M. She got there in time for the alligator siesta hour. Their bellies were full and all you had to do was imagine the snoring and pretty soon the air sounded like hundreds of buzz saws.

The men who worked there were all pretty skeptical, especially when they saw her camera. "What are you, some kind of tourist?" one of them asked.

She just smiled at them and figured it wasn't the best time

to begin an explanation of photorealism. "Can I see the 'gators up close?" she asked.

"Sure," the man said. "We can give you close. Just follow me."

She spent the next two hours snapping pictures of alligators lounging on rocks, sleeping three deep, or sleeping with snout sticking out of the water. It was like walking around in her exercise class when she had to leave early: she had to step around all the alligators they were so many under her feet. Just in case she did step on one, or one hadn't eaten its fill, the man followed her with several pieces of equipment and a running commentary on what she should do in case.

"In case the 'gator open his jaw, don't step inside."

"In case the 'gator wag his tail at you, don't bend down and pet him."

"In case you get a notion to pick up one of them baby 'gators, don't."

"And in case a 'gator start chasing you, don't run away. He can outrun a human every time, and when he catch you, you'll have less strength to fight him. Might as well let him catch you, then hit him on the snout, hit him right there on the snout. He'll get stunned for a minute and let go. Now of course, ma'am, I don't know a living soul who'd willingly let a 'gator catch him, but it's just something to ponder as we walk around here."

The artist couldn't avoid hearing the man muffling a laugh as he gave her his advice.

*

Alligator fact: The Yearling Restaurant near Cross Creek, home of Marjorie Kinnan Rawlings, serves alligator meat, broiled, fried, or steamed.

Alligator fact: Eduardo Alligator was a logo for alligator purses in the 1940s. Eduardo was stamped inside the purse. He wore a straw hat, and carried an alligator purse in one hand, and a cane looped over his paw in the other. He was standing on his two back feet.

Alligator fact: Alligators were on the endangered species list for years, but have made such a comeback they are being grown on farms like corn.

Alligator fact: They migrate through city streets, and everyone leaves them pretty much alone.

Alligator fact: Alligators can outrun a human for a good distance, as the man on the farm said. If an alligator is chasing you, use the same advice farmers give for bulls: climb a tree.

*

Gotta watch out that 'gator   watch out   watch out.

*

This is a story about alligators. So there's no room left to talk about sharks, except to say that when you look out on the Gulf of Mexico and see whitecap waves, a few of them could be shark tails and fins you're seeing. Sharks come in close to shore and scope out the bathers. The view from a helicopter shows dozens of sharks weaving in and out of people doing the Australian crawl, the side stroke, the butterfly, and the dead man's float.

The Bachelors

THE BACHELORS COME to our door, piling up thick as the Tampa heat outside, gabbing, doffing their Panama hats, crooning songs under their breath, songs they want to sing to beautiful women. So far they have been unlucky, and they only sing to each other, practicing, hoping.

"If I didn't know better, I'd think they were courting you," my husband says.

It's true they bring me flowers and assorted gifts, but only because I feed them when they saunter in around dinner time. Sometimes three or four bachelors at once will be sitting around our table, sucking on chicken bones, gulping a beer, licking their fingers where a napkin would do just fine, and belching. Now I've heard that belching is a form of praise for the host, and they've obviously heard that too, but they have gotten their countries mixed up, perhaps their continents and even hemispheres.

"Help me, Laurel," the bachelor Daniel says. "Help me find the one I love, the one who will be true to me, who will love me forever." His beard is bushy, electrified.

"Does she have to be beautiful?" I ask.

"What else?"

"Beauty is only skin deep," I remind him.

"But it's the part you see," he tells me.

At some point in the evening we play cards. I tell their fortunes. They hunger for the queen of hearts, go home sad if she does not appear for them.

"Read my palm," another bachelor named Ron asks.

In school I tell my young students they carry their lives in their hands. I take Ron's hand and turn it over. The skin is soft, unused, the canyons of his hand crooked and short. I know that his life will be easy and brief, like a birthday candle.

"What can I tell you," I say to him, "that you do not already know?" We exchange significant looks and he says, "Laurel, of course – how could I have not realized?"

Finally the bachelors leave for the night as they always must. Ron adjusts his hat carefully so the night breeze will not catch it along with his ponytail toupee and take it out over Tampa Bay, fodder for sharks or a plaything for dolphins. Daniel straps on his guitar, announcing his plans to serenade a woman this very night.

"Isn't that old fashioned?" the bachelor with the toupee asks.

"Even a little fuddy-duddy," my husband says, smiling.

"What do you think, Laurel?" Daniel the guitarist asks.

"I think that it's a beautiful night for music, and that I will now go take a bath, sprinkling the water with some of the hibiscus petals from the flowers that you were so kind to bring." They smile at me as I smooth down my dress with the maps of Florida on it.

*

One bachelor is an especially good friend. Some nights he simply will not leave with the rest. He sits on our porch, the outdoors crowded with the night music of crickets, and he slips the silver harmonica to his lips and plays jazz tunes into the moonless dark. His name is Nathaniel. My husband calls him Nate, but I prefer the rhythm of the full name. He wears a Panama hat and wild shorts with flowers dancing everywhere and a shirt open to his belly button.

"All he needs is a gold chain around his neck to complete the look," my husband says.

Yes, he is a little jealous that Nathaniel can make me laugh, but he and Nate are good friends. During the day they collaborate on screen plays and dream about big bucks and easy street once they sell to Hollywood.

Nathaniel eventually goes home, as all the bachelors do. We have not yet been to his house in Sulphur Springs, a section of Tampa dense with vegetation, and Spanish moss clinging to oaks. He tells us he's somewhat of a hermit, until he met us, that is. He spends most of his time practicing judo and raising his two boys, who were left stranded in California.

Nathaniel talks to me on the phone, excited, doing a kind of sniffle-snort to clear his sinuses. In the background is a large, barking dog. "This woman I met is beautiful, wonderful, oh god, what did I do to deserve this? Man, I've got to do something about the bedrooms here. I told the boys they're just going to have to bunk in together so I can have a room. How the hell could I ask this woman to stay when I just sleep on the couch? The damn couch doesn't even open up. What a trip."

I trail my fingers through my fuzzy blonde hair, trying to figure this out. "So you went to her house?" I ask.

"No, we were at my place. We rolled off the couch onto the rug. Of course it was a little scratchy. I told those boys they better stay put in their rooms. God, she is a gorgeous woman."

"Where'd you meet her?"

"She's a nurse. You know, in the alcohol abuse program. She was assigned to me. I'm her pet project."

"You want to bring her to dinner?" I ask.

"No, actually, well, I was wondering if you and Tom would come here for eats."

"You cook?"

"Hey, don't give me so much grief. I have a family, you know. What'dya think, we do take out every night?"

We go to his house, which is pink stucco Spanish style with a white tile roof and shag carpet in the living room. The dog with the enormous bark looks like a wolf, but has a very unwolf-like name of Pepper. One of the sons is vacuuming the dining room while we are still in the living room. "So this is a bachelor pad," Tom whispers to me. He sits down on the couch which is

Nathaniel's bed, and a black cat jumps out of the cushions. The dog lunges for the cat, and the cat leaps onto Nathaniel and digs into his shoulder, just as he is walking in from the kitchen with a woman who is beautiful and blonde, tall and slender.

"Sayanora, damn it." Nathaniel peels the cat off his body and flings it across the room. The wolf hunches down, ready to play. Nathaniel snaps his fingers. "Watch this."

We all look fascinated as Pepper opens his mouth. I'm impressed with his huge white teeth. Sayanora the cat slowly puts his head inside, and Pepper closes his mouth. "Do something," I say to Tom. But then the mouth opens and the cat inches out and shakes off, begins washing his face.

"The most famous cat act in Sulphur Springs," Nathaniel says. "Oh, this is Dawn. Dawn, this is Laurel and Tom."

We sit in the kitchen while Nathaniel stir fries in a dented, scorched wok. It's the only thing he knows how to cook that resembles dinner party food, he tells us. The two boys take their plates and eat in their rooms. The wolf presses his head from lap to lap, hoping for a hand-out. During dinner Nathaniel and Tom plan out their newest screenplay. "We definitely need a car chase," Nathaniel says.

"Why give in to crass commercialism?" Tom asks.

"That's what sells. It doesn't have to last long – just a few squealing brakes."

After dinner we listen to Nathaniel tell stories about his time in the merchant marines, about how he struggled to earn a black belt in judo, about living half-crazed in L.A. writing and carousing. The L.A. story includes dinner with a famous porn queen. He was sitting next to her at a round table in a restaurant, and she was obviously with the man sitting on her other side, but her hand made a grab for Nathaniel's lap, "which surprised the hell out of me" he says with a grin, sniffing hard to clear his sinuses. His sons hang around the perimeter of the living room, rolling their eyes at his stories, but listening too, laughing with us. The woman Dawn gives Nathaniel a neck rub during some of the stories. She does not tell any of her own.

"Yeah, things are going really well with Dawn," Nathaniel tells me over the next few weeks on the phone. And the writing's going well. I think she must be an inspiration. My agent sold three articles."

"Is she a morning person?" I ask.

"How'd you know?"

"Just a guess, from her name." I laugh at this, but Nathaniel seems to think there's something to it, like maybe her name Dawn caused her to become a morning person.

The bachelors continue to come over, supping with us, telling gossip. As they drift up the path to our door, I throw open my arms to welcome them.

"Joey's ex met him at the door with a shotgun," Daniel says, strumming his guitar.

Ron smooths down his ponytail. "I heard that Mike's going to be a free agent soon."

"Does that mean Monica will be available?"

"Naw. I think she's moving up the coast to Pensacola to stay with relatives. Too bad – she was a lot better looking than Mike."

They laugh. "Sorry, Laurel, this kind of talk isn't very interesting to you."

"Has anyone heard from Nathaniel?" I ask. "We haven't seen him around lately."

"He dropped that bombshell he was dating, you know, the nurse from rehab," Daniel tells me.

When the bachelors leave, I phone Nathaniel. "We haven't seen you around," I say.

"I've been busy. It seems as if I have a million articles to do. My agent is bugging me all the time. I guess I should be happy."

"How's your life going?"

"Fine. How's yours?"

"I mean your love life, Nathaniel."

He sniffs and snorts. "Oh that. Well, I'm seeing a crazy woman named Jana. She trains dolphins for a living. You ought to see her. She gets right into the tank with those beasts. She works at a little place over in St. Pete on the beach. There's a dolphin show and she's the trainer."

"So there's no more Dawn?"

"She got, how shall I say, too clingy. She even started telling the boys what to do. Man, I couldn't take it."

We meet Jana soon after, dripping wet in her bikini and goggles. She walks along the side of the tank and the dolphins follow her. She bends down and talks Dolphin to them. "Fa-fa," she says, and tosses fish in their mouths.

Each time the woman changes, Nathaniel decides to have us over for the stir-fry dinner. The woman seem to change every two months, and Nathaniel varies his reasons:

"Too possessive, kicked in her sleep,

kinky beyond what even I look forward to,

had false teeth that fell out on the pillow,

fell asleep reading my novel,

had wanderlust eyes whenever we went out to eat."

The excuses pile up, and when he reaches for a new one with the latest love lost, I suggest, "Maybe you're not ready to settle down."

"Oh, man, am I glad you said that, Laurel. No, really, I've been telling myself that I should settle down, for the boys' sakes, as well as mine. I like to be with a woman regular, if you know what I mean, but I feel worn out with them after a while. That's it. I'm not ready to settle down."

*

Nathaniel joins us again at the supper table. When he is there, we know he's in between women. When he's with us, he engulfs the conversation. We sit back and listen to his stories. He tells us about the wolf Pepper one night. "Man, that dog considered himself the dominant male of the house. It got so bad, I had to do something."

"Nathaniel," I interrupt. "I guess if you have a wolf that considers itself the dominant male, that it makes sense to do something."

"Yeah," he says.

"Most people would take the animal to obedience school – is that what you did?" I persist. The bachelors and Tom chuckle.

Picturing Nathaniel at obedience school with Pepper the wolf in among poodles and terriers is ridiculous.

"Oh, I took him to obedience school, all right," he says. "But it wasn't anywhere I had to pay money. Man, that dog was sick. He took to growling at me. It was like I couldn't walk into the bathroom without hearing this undertone of growling. One night I had it. Man. 'Enough's enough,' I shouted, and I flipped him on the rug. It took him by surprise, all right." He stops to clear his sinuses and then goes on. "We rolled around on the floor, and he was baring his teeth at me and growling, so I went for his throat. Dogs understand that. I exposed his throat and made as if I were going to sink my teeth in. Right away he stops growling. When I finally let up my hold, I bared my teeth at him and growled some. He was so surprised he started whimpering. Man, I didn't know what I was doing. I just knew I couldn't stand being growled at in my own house. So I kept growling. You know what he did? He rolled over on his back with his legs up in the air. The boys saw the whole thing and they'll tell you it's true. The dog exposed his belly to me, and I was top dog in the house."

*

As each woman in his life evaporates, Nathaniel takes on causes. When he's not writing or over at our house huddling with the other bachelors, he watches TV:

> Dear Tom Brokaw,
> You don't know this, but I watch your program every night. During last night's broadcast you used five split infinitives. You said 'everyone in *their* right minds,' and you misused the verbs lie and lay. What kind of role model are you setting for America? I urge you to become more aware of your sloppy copy and delivery.
> Looking for improvement,
Nathaniel Sharps

I discover the letter on the hamper in his bathroom. "You didn't really send this," I say.

"Not only did I send it," Nathaniel says, jumping up from his couch. "But read this and weep." He rummages through some papers on his desk. He hands me a sheet with official-looking letterhead.

Dear Mr. Sharps:
You will be pleased to know that we are now giving the news copy an extra grammar check at . . .

I don't read any further. "I suppose Jennings and Rather are next," I say.

"Don't encourage him," Tom says. We smile at each other as Nathaniel carefully folds the letters and places them in an envelope.

"Let's get serious," Tom says.

"Proper speech is serious," Nathaniel says.

"I know. I know. I mean another kind of serious. I've got a synopsis with me I'd like you to look at."

"Will it make money?"

"It has a car chase and a dolphin rescue in it."

"Oh yeah? I guess I'll take a look at it."

*

How Nathaniel comes to live with us, I'm not exactly sure. But there he is one day on our doorstep hugging a large color TV and telling his one son left at home to get the door. It has something to do with mortgage payments and no checks from the agent recently. He sweeps our little black and white TV off its perch, sets his color model just so, and asks me for glass cleaner.

They are here to stay it seems. Pepper the wolf lives outside under the avocado tree and constantly wraps his rope around the trunk. There is no more Sayanora the cat. The other bachelors drop by, amazed to learn of Nathaniel's misfortune. "What are you going to do now?" Mike, the newest bachelor at our table, asks.

"I guess I'm going to sleep so I don't have to put up with your stupid-ass questions," Nathaniel says.

"Touchy, touchy," Mike says.

"Read our fortunes," Daniel says, when Nathaniel and his son have safely disappeared.

"It's not right for cards tonight," I say. "But I can do something."

I go in the kitchen and come back with a whole bowl of fortune cookies wrapped in cellophane.

"Those things are worthless," Mike says.

"No one believes them," Ron says. He has exchanged his ponytail toupee for a model that is short and slicked back, sort of how I envision Dracula.

"Don't be such cynics," I answer. "Try one."

We all watch as Mike bites open a packet. He crushes the cookie and pulls out the white paper ribbon. "The love of your life is closer than you think" he reads. Suddenly the activity at the table picks up. Hands reaching for fortune cookies create a loud crinkle of noise.

"Keep it down out there," Nathaniel yells from the guest room.

Later Tom and I lie in bed staring into the dark. "What the hell is that noise?" he asks.

"It sounds like a bubbling brook," I mumble.

We listen for a while longer. "It's raining out now," Tom says. "Funny, there was no rain in the forecast."

As we listen, the rain turns into ocean surf. We both sit up and ease off the bed. The ocean is coming from inside the guest room. We knock on the door.

His son Rick squints out through a narrow opening. "Shhhhush. My dad doesn't like to be disturbed once he turns on his white noise machine. He can't go to sleep without it. He hates to be woken up worse than anything."

One day while I'm hanging clothes on the line in the yard and wishing for the first time that our house was not a haven for tag-along bachelors, Nathaniel joins me, handing me clothes. He mentions that he's been daydreaming about a girl from Hillsborough High School that he always admired but never actually dated.

"But that must have been at least twenty years ago," I say.

"So? I wonder if she's still here in Tampa. Vicky was into music, and she surprised everyone when she married a stock broker and didn't become a professional songbird. She had the voice for it."

He goes inside, makes a single phone call, and has a one day courtship in which he somehow convinces a woman he hasn't seen in twenty years to let him move into her plush condo on the Bayshore. I learn that the wolf will be living inside also.

From then on, Nathaniel drops out of the bachelor gatherings. He and Vicky move on, to Georgia and then to Washington State. They've married by now, he writes, and he thinks he likes being married again. They move back to the south quickly though because the weather out there gets to Nathaniel's sinuses. He writes and calls, but we don't see him for a long time.

One day I'm by the clothesline pinning up blouses, and he appears in the distance. He walks across the yard, surveying the overgrown palms and fallen seed pods from the orchid tree. "You really should do something about this yard, Laurel," he says.

I drop my clothespin bag and open my arms for a hug. Way behind him on the sidewalk is a large old rusty American car of uncertain vintage and color.

"I'm just here for the weekend – I'm going to join G. Gordon Liddy's survival school, or whatever the hell it's called. An editor wants me to do a piece on it. You guys still married? Oh, hell, don't even answer that."

"How about yourself?" I ask. Our eyes meet and dart away.

"I guess it depends on who you ask. Vicky thinks we are, and I'm not so sure about that. Then again, the state of Georgia probably has a different view. Anyway, my agent called and said I should completely avoid the Georgia boundary line for a while. Something about a subpoena and men looking like Jack Webb waiting to ask me if I'm Nate Sharps, Married Man . . . "

"Stop, I've heard enough." I snap a clothespin at him.

"Then let's go inside and get me some iced tea, and rev up the air conditioner the way you know I like it. I'll just get my things from the car, including the Great Pyrenees mastodon mongrel mutt I've been breeding in the trunk." I hear him laugh and do his sniffle/snort as he lopes back across the yard.

*

Nathaniel is long gone when the new year begins. The bachelors sit around the table and I throw the tiles for their *I Ching*. "Have a question in mind," I counsel, "and don't change it once the tiles are down." I read their hexagrams and the commentary that follows. For Daniel: *Po*/Splitting apart. For Mike: *Lu*/The Wanderer. And Ron: *Ta Yu*/Possession in Great Measure. When the phone rings, I am not surprised.

"Yeah, it's Nathaniel." He sniffs into the phone. "Things aren't going too well. Man. You know, Laurel, how it is sometimes."

"I wish you were here," I say.

"Give me something, Laurel. Anything. A quick fix you can send through this wire right now."

Quickly I tell Tom to act as proxy, and explain to Nathaniel that he needs to think of a question for the new year. "We're throwing the *I Ching*," I say.

Tom picks six tiles. "Oh, you've drawn *Ching*/The Well." I read him the commentary, the image and the lines. I end with: "Six at the top means:/One draws from the well/Without hindrance./It is dependable./Supreme good fortune."

"I feel better already," Nathaniel says, but his flat voice belies him. In my imagination I press the lines of his face together into a smile. Who knows, maybe we do have abilities to sculpt one another telepathically. Behind me as I talk on the phone, the bachelors in my life place bets on who among them will stumble down the aisle first.

The World Traveler

I AM WAITING to greet my mother. It is her annual pilgrimage down to Florida. Every other passenger is off the plane. Men with vacuum cleaners are walking onto the plane. Even the flight crew is off. I shift from one foot to another. I always try to stand with my weight on both feet at once. I am afraid of becoming asymmetrical.

Sam comes up behind me. He trimmed his beard this morning, and there is a bare patch under his chin. He left the little red hairs scattered in the sink like leaves and went to watch a basketball game on TV. But then he raked them up at half-time.

"Where is she?" I ask.

"You know she's slow."

Do I know she's slow. Years ago, when her body still cooperated with her, she was slow. It took her eons to get ready for work in the morning. Her bedtime ritual was to lay out all her clothes, her gabardine skirt, her white blouse, her underwear that was the size of bloomers – she hated anything tight – her nylons and garter belt, her full slip. My mother never wore a brassiere. She was small and compact and had trouble getting her breath even back then, so everything she wore had to be loose on her. The only thing that ever changed was the color of her skirt: from gray to navy blue to black to forest green. She has worn dentures since I was in kindergarten. They cause her to eat slowly, making her appear to savor every bite. Her whole life has become a crawl.

*

My mother has her own wheels now. It's the first time I've seen her emerge from the airplane via chair transport. She is giving the man who is pushing the chair her recipe for asparagus soup. She is talking to him with her head tilted back. When my mother eats asparagus, she cuts off the hard ends and freezes them. Then she simmers them in a broth to make soup. She has discovered this trick herself and is proud of it. The young black man pushing the chair is not even making a pretense of listening. He is speaking into a walkie talkie. My mother is so proud of her trick of saving the asparagus ends. It's like her orange juice trick: she squeezes a real orange into a quart of concentrated juice. It makes it taste as if it's all freshly squeezed. My mother clings to these tricks. They are her magic show.

Naturally my mother is glad to see me. The first thing she says is, "Rachel, I didn't think I'd make it." We hug, and I can feel her crying against me. When I don't say anything, she says, "I really thought last year was my final visit." I am still hugging her, but I feel motion. She is fishing in her pocket to peel a piece of Kleenex off the wad she always has. Her hair is auburn this time. It is cut short and has gray roots inching out from the crown.

She is draped in her perennial grays: gray houndstooth rain/ shine coat with a gray furry lining that zips out, gray muffler around her shoulders, clear plastic rain boots that have turned gray from Chicago's winter slush. Once my mother painted all the walls in our house charcoal gray. She made curtains out of gray mattress ticking. I have never been able to wear anything gray without feeling that all the color is being sucked out of the world.

*

The car ride home, across the bridge from Tampa to St. Petersburg usually indicates how the visit will go.

"Did you get a new stove yet?" my mother asks.

"No," Sam says. "We're still saving for it."

"Don't be silly," my mother says. "I told you to buy a stove and put it on my Sears charge. From the time you've been married you've been cooking on that rusty piece of junk." My mother is a queen in the front seat. Ever since we bought a two-door miniature foreign car she has gotten the front seat because she is no longer able to fold up her body like a Swiss army knife. I have taken my place in the back. The territory is familiar. Since I am short, I have spent my entire life in the back seat of cars, usually in the middle with my feet up on the hump.

"Sam doesn't do the cooking, Mom." I clear my throat. I can feel my voice getting stretched, like a rubber band. Sam glances in the rear-view mirror, and my mother tilts her head in a backward pose. "Sam doesn't care if the stove's a rusty piece of junk," I continue. "Besides, we don't like to buy on time. We like to pay cash."

My mother is right. Every time I open the oven door a flake of rust falls out from some internal organ.

*

My mother is fragile, like soap bubbles. She fooled me for many years though. She has big hands, and feet that were solidly placed on the ground and knew where they were going. After the divorce, she made the journey to the basement every winter morning. Those large hands grasped a shovel and fed coal into the fiery mouth of the great gray furnace. I lay in bed, two flights up, listening to the scraping noise of the shovel on the coal bin floor reverberating up through the heat register. I had long brown hair, and when I washed it in winter I would lie on my back on the register and fan out my hair and let it dry.

Now my mother's hands tremble when she writes. She leans on a cane when she walks. Her feet take cautious steps, as if they each want to go in a different direction.

*

My mother is a traveler in her mind alone. She has gone to distant shores and explored the terrain of foreign lands in the books she reads. Her friends know where to park their used *National Geographics*. She has had a non-stop subscription to *Holiday* for twenty-five years. She is past seventy. Her emphysema is unwinding her. She visits us with hope. Florida is a long way from Illinois, and it means she can still get around. A friend of hers has dubbed her the World Traveler. That's because several years back she flew to Hawaii with friends. Many years before a gypsy had predicted that she would cross a large body of water. My mother clung to this prediction, thinking it meant she would get to Paris. When she went to Hawaii, she knew the prediction had come true, and she knew she would never get to Paris.

She has hardly ever left Chicago. But she got on a train when I was in graduate school and visited me in Ohio. She came with my Aunt Alicia, her older sister. Alicia is a tiny woman, formed into a body that had grown crookedly. When I was eight and a half I passed Alicia in height. My mother is only 5'4" but looks tall beside her. Alicia has been to Europe several times and to New York uncountable times. "Your father could have taken me to New York on a business trip," my mother always says, "but he chose not to." Their visit did not start off well. My mother didn't like climbing – I lived on a high second floor. Aunt Alicia was afraid of cats – there were two.

I introduced them to Sam, then my boyfriend. "Doesn't he ever go home?" Aunt Alicia asked late the first evening. The answer was no, but I told them "eventually" hoping to buy time. They regarded him as inorganic material until he offered to go out and get a bottle of brandy. That seemed to please them. They elevated him to some sort of living creature. They were women who had been without men for years. I guess they were surprised to be around one. "He has such red hair," my mother said. "I don't think he's Jewish," she added, raising an eyebrow at Alicia and listening for me to say, "Oh yes he is" and make everything all right. I didn't say anything. They spent the long weekend drinking their brandy and dodging cats. They didn't want to go out – the stairs were a problem, even for Alicia. We did go out once, to lunch. Afterwards we went to the town courthouse. Sam and I had heard there were displays of prominent trials of the last hundred years. We took my mother to see a finger of a murder victim pickled in a jar. Aunt Alicia sat on a bench and refused to participate.

*

My mother moves into our lives on her visits to Florida. She comes to my aerobic dance class and watches me do chicken walks, airplanes and rope pulls to a fast beat. She and Sam, half in their pajamas, throw coats around themselves, and go to an all-night food store at 2 A.M. They sneak back in with a bag of ice cream and cookies. For my mother it is an adventure.

My mother's body is disappearing. Each year it is five or ten pounds less than the year before. The cortisone she takes has something to do with the weight loss. I concoct milkshakes. She sips them, never finishing them. I bake chicken. She eats a wing. But one thing that is always present: a plate of bread. There must be a plate of bread, with slices stacked high, protected by the heel. It is the standard table ornament during my mother's visit. I make large bowls of potatoes: mashed, scalloped, baked in foil skins, and my mother's favorite – new potatoes in their red jackets.

"Eat more," I command.

"I can't," my mother says. "I'll eat what I want. Do you have any chocolate?"

I retrieve the jumbo Hershey bar from the refrigerator. I have been waiting to spring it on her.

"Oh my," she says. "This will last my whole visit." She daintily breaks off one square and pops it in her mouth

*

She attends an opening of an art gallery in Tampa. She inspects each painting closely, declaring that our friend Ted's paintings are the best. She has always been loyal. After her tour of the gallery, she sits at the front desk, the only place there is a chair. Sam and I walk around. My mother is on her own for a brief moment in Tampa, Florida, holding on to her cane for support. People ask her questions. She is taken for the gallery manager.

She answers the questions. When I come to the front of the gallery again, I find my mother talking to a young man in a white suit and Panama hat. He is sitting on the desk, and he has a cane that he is leaning on. At first I think it's my mother's cane, but then I see it has a parrot carved on the handle. They are talking about their canes, where they got them and why they have to use them. The man is smoking a joint. My mother tells me the name of his rare disease. I try to signal her that maybe she is being put on. But they go back to talking. They talk almost the whole time we are there. Before we leave, she convinces someone to buy a painting that Ted did. She hands out membership brochures. She shakes hands with the man in the white suit. She is the hit of the show. When we get outside she confides in me that she thinks the man in the white suit was high on something.

*

At night my mother sleeps a room away from us, separated by a tiny hallway. I listen to her snoring, which sounds like gasping for air. When things are too quiet, when I can't hear the breathing, I slide down from our iron-framed bed. I go to my mother's room and push open the door to listen. I can hear the breathing now, which has momentarily become calm. I am checking to make sure my mother is still alive. I take a silent breath of air, the same air that my mother finds so elusive. I am checking to make sure my mother is alive. I do this every night.

*

My mother does certain things that drive me wild. She travels to Florida with ten bars of Ivory Soap – bath size – nested in her suitcase. She brings boxes of Kleenex, wedging them in amongst her shoes. She is afraid I will not have enough soap, and there can never be enough Kleenex. She does her laundry by hand. She makes me go out and buy a bucket that she can wash in. She becomes a peasant in a village somewhere in Europe, standing by my kitchen sink. I go shopping to avoid seeing the ritual of laundry. She refuses all offers to have her clothes taken to the laundromat. I come home to find her voluminous underwear stuck on the shrubbery in my yard, and her dresses hanging from low branches of trees. The plastic clothesline is too high. Or it isn't clean enough. Or it is in the shade.

*

We stop in a bar where there is live music. A friend of ours has studied in clown school, and now he is Bartholomew the Clown who does magic tricks at the bar. He has two furry animals that he uses in part of his act. They are reminiscent of a ferret and a skunk, but it's hard to tell what they are for certain. He holds them in his hands and walks around and lets people pet them. They scurry up his arm, and nibble at his shirt, and drink out of people's beer mugs. One afternoon we were there and someone complained about there being live animals in a place that serves food. Bartholomew the Clown put them in a cage and took them out to his car. Sam became distraught. He couldn't stand the idea of the animals being in the hot car. A friend of mine let me in on the secret soon after: the animals are puppets. I couldn't believe it. They move so realistically. Sam refused to accept it. But the next time I saw the act, I looked at the animals. Of course they are not real. Their eyes are glassy and chipped.

We take my mother to the bar and order dinner while she sips a whiskey sour. Bartholomew begins making his rounds to the tables. He has the skunk in his hand and he comes up to my mother. She laughs at him. The skunk sniffs around at her drink. She slaps Bartholomew on the arm in a friendly way, and says, "You can't fool me – that isn't real – but you're good, you're very good." I am very disappointed. I try to tell my mother that the animal is real. She won't have it.

"It is," I say.

"Come on, Rachel," she says. "I've lived too long. Don't keep saying that." She is clutching a piece of Kleenex, and the tufts of white are poking between her fingers.

"It is alive," I say. "Tell her it is, Sam."

"Enough," my mother says, reaching for her fork to finish eating. Her hand trembles as she puts it to her mouth.

Sam gives me a look that would pop corn.

It is the last day of my mother's visit. "Hurry and finish," I say, "and we can still make happy hour at the Pier." My voice creaks with sudden desperation.

Safe Passage

MY MOTHER SITS in her wheelchair in the dining room pointing her cane at one of the cats. She moves the cane back and forth. The cat pounces on the end of the cane. "Rachel," my mother calls.

I am sitting two feet away at the table. I explain to her that if she wiggles the cane, the cat will pounce. I have explained this to her a dozen times since she has arrived two days ago, and hundreds of times counting all her other visits.

A white crumpled piece of Kleenex hits the floor. My mother and I both look down. The cat is eyeing it with interest. I reach down and pull the cat away. I tell my mother to try picking it up. She gives me a disgusted look. She makes her disgusted look by pinching her lips together and making the corners of her mouth go down.

My mother has a contraption we have dubbed a picker-upper. She received it during one of her hospital stays. It's long with squeeze handles and two rubber suction cups on the end that resemble the suction cup darts my brother and I used to play with.

She takes her picker-upper and aims the ends near the Kleenex and squeezes the handles. Then she slowly lifts it up. "God-dammit," she says. There is no Kleenex on the end. "I'm no good with machinery. Can't you just pick it up for me? Come on!"

Later, Sam and I are in bed. My feet are scrunched under his legs for warmth. My body is heavy and my eyes are closed, but I am not asleep. I listen to Sam's breathing, and to the scuffling going on in the living room. The door closes.

"Changing of the guard," Sam mumbles.

"I thought you were asleep," I whisper.

He doesn't answer. I hear a voice in Sam's study, where my mother is set up in a hospital bed, with a huge canister of oxygen looming in the corner and a portable toilet by the desk. The voice is saying hello to my mother. Sam and I listen, trying to catch a name, to figure out if it is a nurse we recognize. She will be gone by morning and someone else will be in her place.

We lie in our bed. a few feet from my mother and a stranger, able to hear everything through the louvered door of our bedroom. There have been so many nurses in the last forty-eight hours that it seems as if my mother has been here for many days.

The next day is the same. My mother sits in her wheelchair in the dining room. She is afraid to get out of it, even though she was starting to walk back in Chicago. More therapy is what she needs, I was told. And a warm climate. We are in Florida and it is warmer than Chicago even though it is winter here too. She likes the nurse who is here today – she is large and hefty, and when she helps my mother from the wheelchair to the portable toilet in the study, my mother does not say anything – she lets herself be lifted. She won't let me touch her. She is afraid I will drop her. She might be right. I don't do well with bundles of any sort. In the past she never even trusted me to give her a boost out of the car when she couldn't quite stand up from the low car seat.

The procession of nurses continues. Helen, Bebe, Maria, Dottie. They sign a sheet of paper at the end of their shift. Sam drives one of them home when a ride doesn't materialize. They bathe my mother, prepare her food, or watch me dish out some of the food I have made, wash her dishes, help her onto the portable toilet. We try to get the wheelchair outside so my mother can enjoy the sun. The stoops by each door make this a major event. The nurse mentions that we need to install ramps. I flinch, trying to wiggle the chair down the stoop. My mother is not supposed to be in a wheelchair. She is supposed to be walking by now. But the truth is, my mother cannot even lift a telephone receiver by herself she is so weak.

"I'm worried," I tell Sam on the phone. He is at work.

"She's got to cooperate," he says. "She's got to start walking."

"She doesn't want to," I say. I take a deep breath. Up till now I have been fooling myself. My mother keeps saying how much she wants to walk, but she clings to the arms of her wheelchair with any strength she has left.

"You have to do something about this, Rachel," he says. "It can't go on."

I know he is right. I have to go back to work soon. Sometimes I have to be out of the house for twelve hours at a time.

My mother is in bed now even though the doctor says she should sit in a chair during the day. She somehow convinced the nurse to put her back in the bed. She is watching *The Philadelphia Story* with Katharine Hepburn and Cary Grant. The nurse is in a lounge chair with a movie star magazine. It has been so long since I have seen a movie magazine that I am amazed they are still being printed. I thought only teenagers read them, but this woman is at least twenty-five. It makes me angry that the nurse is sitting and reading a magazine even though I know there is nothing really to do. I think she should try to find something to do. I stand in the doorway and finally ask the nurse named Barbara if she will make my mother some lunch. Then I take her place in the lounge chair. I find myself getting wrapped up in the movie, hoping that the commercial doesn't come on. My mother has a grin on her face. She is watching Cary Grant be charming to the mother and sister. I want to yell at my mother for being in bed, but I promise myself I won't even mention it because there are more important things to talk about.

The commercial comes on. I have my speech prepared: about my going back to work, and how costly the nursing service is – all her money will be eaten up in no time if we continue with it – and how the doctor said she can't be left alone, not even for a few minutes. After I give my speech, I take up the movie magazine and begin thumbing through it.

The movie begins again. My mother and I are both silent. We are staring at the images on the screen, but I am not sure if we are concentrating. I hear a muffled sound. My mother is crying. I don't know what to do. I put down the magazine. She holds out her hand to me. I go over and sit on the edge of her bed. "I know what you're telling me," she says.

I glance at her oxygen tube, watching it snake under the sheet.

"I know," she says. "There's no money for nurses, so ... "

"There isn't," I say. "They're too expensive."

"I don't want to leave here," she says. "I don't want to be anywhere else but here."

"But starting next week, I have to go back to work. Besides, I can't lift you."

"No, I don't want you to lift me ... " My mother's voice trails off. "But what will happen to me?"

I look at her and she looks at me. Her hand grasps mine. It is papery. It feels like dusty autumn leaves. I lean down and we hug each other. "Please try to get up after the movie," I say.

"I'll try," my mother says.

*

I am driving across town. It is a warm winter morning. A woman stands at a bus stop with an exotic sun hat that has a built-in umbrella sprouting from the top and shading her. I stop at a light. My mother would laugh at this woman, talk about her get-up, but like this woman, my mother also wears a huge pair of sunglasses over her regular glasses. This is a city without snow, far from my midwestern roots. The closest we come to ice is an occasional hail storm, and twice I have woken in the morning to see the grass white: frosted over from freezing temperatures. Last night I heard that it was below zero in Chicago. "Aren't you lucky?" I will say to my mother. "You're out of that cold."

I turn down the road to Shore Acres. It is a subdivision in the city. It is built on landfill and is prone to flooding. It takes me a half hour to drive to the yellow house with the tile roof. It is where my mother is living now.

When I ring the bell a woman shorter than my 5'2" height opens the door. She is chunky, wearing lavender polyester Bermuda shorts and a tank top. She has metal clips poking in her hair. Her name is Dorothy and I have entrusted her with the care of my mother. She grins, says "Hi" the way I said it years ago when I was a camp counselor and I was trying to make myself sound enthusiastic. Her house is a model home with heavy, upholstered furniture and thick carpeting that most people would call luxurious. The decor doesn't appeal to me, but everything is clean and tidy and expensive looking. Dorothy is younger than I am by five years – she is thirty-two, but I think of her as being much older, like an aunt.

"She's in the hallway," Dorothy says.

I walk through the living room and look in the hallway. My mother is standing with a metal walker. A man is behind her saying, "Right foot, now, Iris, right foot." There is a portable oxygen tank on wheels at the end of the hall that has a long feeder tube that runs to my mother's face. I watch my mother put one foot in front of the other in a shuffle. The physical therapist waves to me in a conspiracy even though we have never met. Suddenly my mother looks up. "Oh, Rachel," she says. "This is Joel – he's making me walk."

I roll my eyes to the ceiling. "You *want* to walk," I say. "No one is making you walk, right?"

"Right," my mother says quickly.

Joel seems to have her best interests in mind. He says she'll be walking well in another couple of weeks. He says she is able to do more than she admits to. A little later he has her demonstrate going from her bed to the portable toilet and then to the wheelchair by herself. "She's stronger than she lets on," he assures me. He says this in front of her as if she can't hear.

"Are you satisfied now, Rachel?" she asks.

"This is for you," I say, "not for me."

"I know, but I want you to be satisfied too."

I get a heavy feeling in my stomach. My mother is tapping her right foot, a nervous gesture she has had for years.

*

I visit my mother several times a week, but she never calls me, even though she has a phone in her room at Dorothy's and I have asked her to call, if for no other reason than to give her something to do. When I call her, our conversations are brief. "Dorothy put curlers on my hair today," she tells me. "She told me my hair made me look like a witch the way it was."

I frown on my end of the phone for an instant, but brighten my voice for my mother. "Well, curls will make you feel better." My mother always hated having her hair curled. She has worn her hair short and straight for over twenty-five years.

When Dorothy gets on the phone she tells me my mother is doing a little better today – that she didn't yell so much in her sleep last night. I hadn't known my mother wasn't doing all right, and I didn't know about the yelling at all. Dorothy waits for me to ask about it, but I don't. "We'll bring her around," Dorothy says. "Don't worry. I've had much sicker ones than your mother."

I squirm a little and wonder if Dorothy is talking from the phone in my mother's room or if she is in the kitchen.

Sam drives with me across town on the weekends. We visit my mother in her room. She makes sure the intercom is turned off and then gives me a litany of complaints: she wanted a second glass of wine after dinner and Dorothy wouldn't give it to her; Dorothy yelled at her when she spilled water on the rug; there was so little meat with dinner last night she could have threaded it through a needle.

I am trying to control myself. I want to yell at her that this was the best I could arrange for her. At least she's in a private home with a beautiful room to herself. Sam is sitting in a chair writing something in a notebook. He is taking notes on my mother, chronicling her illness, making the time pass. He hardly says anything during the visits.

"I am trying," my mother says. Her eyes dart back and forth and she taps her foot.

Later, Dorothy comes in and says it's time for her exercises. My mother's face gets stony. "C'mon, Iris, on the bed." Dorothy gestures with her hands as if she is shooing chickens back in a pen.

It takes my mother five minutes to rise from her wheelchair and use the walker over to her bed. Finally she collapses on the mattress. Dorothy attaches ankle weights that the physical therapist has brought over. She instructs my mother to do fifty leg lifts. When she sees Sam's and my horrified looks, she says that the therapist wrote down the instructions the other day, that she's able to do the leg lifts but she tries to cheat so we should watch her. "I'll let you count for her, and don't let her come up short," she says, waving her finger at us. "Go to it, Iris," she says as she leaves the room.

We watch my mother struggle through fifty leg lifts with each leg. I'm not sure I could do that many with weights on and I go to a exercise class. My mother has never done exercise in her life, and I wonder how she can do fifty all of a sudden. On our way out Dorothy says that she will lose the physical therapist benefit on Medicare if she doesn't do the fifty leg lifts twice a day. That's what the therapist estimates she can do, so that's what she has to do to keep the benefits. On other visits weights are attached to my mother's cane and she must lift the cane up and down. The exercise is done to strengthen her arm muscles so she can push herself up more easily.

One afternoon I take my mother out for lunch. She creeps to the car with her walker. Dorothy has said that we can't wheel her in the chair because she needs the walking practice. I strap my mother in the front seat with the belt. We drive around the neighborhood for a while. My mother tells me it feels wonderful to get out of that house.

"Mother . . . " I say. My voice is hard. "I don't want to hear complaints."

"Well, I just had to say it," she says.

For lunch we go to a fast food place that has a drive-through. We get sodas and two orders of fried chicken livers. The livers were suggested by my mother. Dorothy brought some home one night, and my mother claims they are the best food Dorothy has served. I drive to a nearby park and we sit in the car and eat the food. The livers are coated with batter and are congealed in grease. I eat one and my hands and face become smeared with grease. My mother is eating hers without complaint, even thought she doesn't usually like fried food. As I eat, the grease accumulates in my mouth, sticking to my teeth and tongue. My teeth feel furry and I picture this heavy grease clogging my arteries. I have never eaten anything so greasy in my entire life. I can only finish two of the livers. My mother eats all of hers and carefully wipes her face. "They were good," she says.

I reach for my keys to start the car. "Just a minute," my mother says. She takes my hand. Hers is shaking, palsy-like. I have never felt her hand shake before. I am reminded of dusty autumn leaves again as I touch her skin – the veins on the top of her hand are thick and poking out.

"I need to tell you, Rachel – I need to tell you, and you have to listen – I'm not all together – I'm losing control – I think I'm losing my mind."

I am about to get angry at her, to tell her that she's not trying hard enough, but there are tears in her eyes and her hand squeezes mine. I drive her back to Dorothy's and I go inside and get the wheelchair this time to bring my mother in. Part of me says that it is giving in to my mother – how will she get well if we baby her – but another part says that she really needs the chair and no amount of leg lifts will change the situation.

*

Dorothy's call comes early the next morning. I am not surprised to hear from her. She tells me my mother was screaming and crying all night, and she can't have that in her house, that her whole family was disturbed. I tell her I will do something about it as soon as I reach her doctor.

The doctor recommends hospitalization. He arranges for tests and psychiatric care. My relief is immense and I call Dorothy to tell her that my husband and I will be over soon. Sam tucks his notebook in his jacket pocket, as he has each time we have visited my mother.

My mother's whole mood is changed. She is still shaking and distracted, but she seems relaxed. "I can't wait until I get out of here," she says in a stage whisper. I am angry, but sorry for her at the same time. Sam and I manage to get her into the car. She is wearing a red velour robe that I sent her last winter as a present. I had hemmed it before I sent it because I knew it would be too long for her. Dorothy closes the car door and leans her face to the window, looking at me in the back seat. "A rest in the hospital will do her good – she'll be back here in no time – the exercises were really helping." My mother, in the front seat, two inches from Dorothy's face, turns her head away.

As we drive, she sinks deeper and deeper into the seat, almost falling asleep. In the hospital she lists to one side in her wheelchair as we make arrangements in the admitting office. "Get me to a bed," she hisses to me at one point. Finally, we go up to her assigned room. "I've got to lie down," she keeps saying over and over. An elderly man who is a volunteer at the hospital is pushing her wheelchair. Sam and I are carrying her belongings, including her houndstooth rain/shine coat with the fake fur zip out lining that she insisted I bring with us. We get to her room, and we help her onto the bed and she melts into it. "I had to lie down," she says to me, "you'll never know how much I had to lie down." Sam goes to find a drinking fountain. His notebook is open on the end of the bed. The last twenty or so pages contain quotes from my mother – things that she said during our visits to Dorothy's. When I ask Sam about the notations, he only says, "I think we'll find it important . . . later."

We wait in semi-darkness for a nurse to come and ask questions. My mother is asleep, hooked to her oxygen, breathing steadily. I go over and hold her hand. I know she will never go back to Dorothy's. That is over. I sit uneasily on the edge of the bed. I can still feel the grease in my mouth from yesterday. I guaranteed my mother safe passage from her life in Chicago to a new life in Florida after she had a complete collapse. So far it has been a turbulent voyage, and not very safe. I hold her papery hand and wait for the next embarkment.

Coast to Coast

Coast to Coast

Going Under

WHEN MIRIAM ARRIVES in Grand Central Station, she goes to the clock she's supposed to stand by, and watches for someone whose skin resembles a baby's, reasoning that anyone who is reported to be in back-to-the-womb therapy would have smooth skin.

A young man in a coat that makes his body look like a series of stacked sausages comes up to her and says, "Hi, I'm Random Chestnut."

"How did you know who I was?" Miriam asks.

"Intuitive feelings. Vibrations. Julie is one of my best friends from college, and I guess I picked up some kind of genetic overlay – you being cousins and all. Besides, she said you were short, and would have a million suitcases that matched." He looks down significantly at the robins egg blue luggage that goes from the huge papa down to the little round circle of a case that is for make-up, but has leaflets for the convention.

"It's mostly stuff from my publishing company."

"We're going to have a hell of a time on the subway."

"I can afford a cab."

"Are you kidding?"

"No, my company pays for it."

"It's a personal issue with me. I never take cabs."

They bundle onto the subway. So what if they jab people with her suitcases, and so what if a man curses at them for taking up too much room? Miriam becomes an instant pro. She tells the red-faced man that they paid an extra fare for the big suitcase. To the next person who complains, Random says, "They're under five years old, they ride free."

He and Miriam smile at each other. She tries to imagine him scrunched in a fetal position for hours and can't do it. His thick black hair is combed back over his ears and looks set into place for life. And his skin is rough with his heavy beard trying to show through. She begins to look forward to getting to his place: a nice cup of tea, a soak in a tub, and a nap between crisp sheets – maybe she'll try the fetal position for a laugh – and she'll be ready for the evening events at the convention. "I live in Greenwich Village," he says, "nice old building near Washington Square."

And interesting atmosphere. She's glad she decided to stay with Julie's friend instead of at a hotel. What more could she ask for?

*

The building is disappointingly plain from the outside. It looks like a place her Aunt Rose would have lived, and Aunt Rose wouldn't have lived just anywhere. Yellow brick exterior – four floors – new paint around the windows. The hallway is equally plain, and would meet Aunt Rose's coveted approval: well lit and freshly vacuumed. A man in a suit emerges from an apartment and the aroma of homemade bread follows him. "Families," Random explains. "I'm the only single in the whole place. I kind of add zest to their lives. Women are always giving me plates of doughnuts and containers filled with leftovers." As he turns the key in the lock, he says, "I could start a Tupperware business on the side with all the containers I've forgotten to return."

Nothing in all her previous experience, not even the hotel she once lived in which was a grade A flophouse, prepares her for what is behind the door that he opens. Nothing that she knows about him – mainly that he is interested in wombs – prepares her either. He's neatly dressed, hair combed, and she even suspects he uses a dab of after-shave. The hallway inside is dark and musty. Not the kind of musty that happens when you open a little-use drawer, but a kind of old sweaty gym shoe musty. The hallway smells like her brother's gym shoes which were recognizable at forty paces. Suspending impossibility, she almost asks, "Has Mike been here?" but then she trips on something.

"Laundry," Random says. "I'll have to do it sometime." He flicks on a ceiling light and the laundry becomes visible. It is laid out in clumps along the whole hallway, like a flower bed. Everything is wadded up and inside out: sweatshirts doing acrobatic flips with gray and moldy towels, and underwear lying naked and unashamed with spots and flecks for anyone to see. Maybe it will get better. Maybe he let his laundry accumulate by accident. But propagate would be a better word.

To make pleasant conversation, she says, "You must have a lot of clothes to let your laundry go for so long."

"Yeah," he says, "my family always gives me underwear and socks for Christmas and birthdays – they know I hate to do laundry. I mean, it's such a waste of time. Your brain feels like it's in suspended animation while you're sitting there and watching clothes go around and around and around. It's enough to drive you batty."

They end up in a living room barely large enough to sneeze in. It is filled with plant life swarming out of pots and over book shelves. Purple grow lights give the room an eerie feeling. The only window faces a wall of the building next door. But it's always easy to be too critical. There are a couple of chairs and a couch, and a bench in front of the couch with magazines on it, which all add up to a true-to-life living room. "Maybe we can have some tea?" she asks, trying to carry out the first stage of her fantasy.

"Tea?" Random says, in a voice that makes it seem as if tea is not in his experience. "Sure, maybe we can." He heads toward a little room off the living room, but then he backs away and heads across the room to a doorway and opens it. "In a few minutes, okay? Give me a few minutes, and maybe we'll have some tea."

Her suitcases surround her like a fort, and she steps over them and stretches. Then she bends down to see if she can still touch her toes, and practically puts her nose into one of the bowls on the bench. The insides of the bowls are glazed with a greenish tint. Pistachio ice cream or lime jello. The sour smell doesn't give it away. Her hand touches the end of one of the spoons in a bowl, only it doesn't move. Instead, the whole bowl moves. She experimentally lifts the end of a spoon, and the bowl lifts. Her first suspicion was correct. The spoons are glued to the bowls. It is some kind of pop art. That has to be it.

Random must have forgotten about the tea. She peers into the dim space that is the kitchen. It's tiny with no window. Also, there is a peculiar odor – it takes a moment but she recognizes it: the odor of things being left out that have rotted. When the light goes on, the kitchen moves. "Ohhh . . . " she can't hold back a gasp, and it is not a gasp of pleasure. Roaches are everywhere. She can hardly tell the color of the cabinets there are so many roaches. The light doesn't make them run to their hiding places, the way it's supposed to. Their campsites have No Vacancy signs posted. With that much overpopulation, all they can do is scurry around in dizzy circles. "Stay back," she yells, and douses the light. I will never go into that kitchen again, she promises herself. Lumpy bags were piled on the counters, wet with geriatric garbage, spilling their coffee ground and tomato paste guts onto filthy curling linoleum. And where the sink might have been were dozens of plastic containers with the scummy remains of tuna salads and lasagna innocently given to Random by some of the other tenants.

Random emerges from his cocoon in time to tell her that she looks faint, and he'll get her the cup of tea now.

"Oh, no, that's okay." Sampling anything from that room with condemned garbage, and a burnt tongue would be the least of her worries. "I'm just tired from my trip. I really have to get going to the convention."

"At least let me tell you how to get to the Americana." He draws her a little map on the back of a napkin, and tells her which train to ride. Then he sits and smiles at her while she tries to pull the wrinkles out of her suit. She recalls with glowing hatred Julie assuring her that Random has an iron. "Wrinkles," Random says, "they're a losing battle. I surrendered a long time ago." The hands that drew the map for her are wrinkled too, like white raisins. Maybe this womb therapy is backfiring, and making him older.

Somehow she manages to scare enough wrinkles out of her skirt to please even Aunt Rose. She decides subways are for tomorrow and daylight, and hails a cab at the corner. At the hotel the first thing she finds out is there are no more guest rooms – full up from the convention.

No time to dwell on her good luck. She signs in for the convention and supervises the setting up of her booth to display the books from her company.

*

It is very late when she returns to Greenwich Village and the apartment that reminds her of three-day-old unrefrigerated macaroni salad. She finds herself facing the plain brick building. The question, "Where will I sleep?" hits her for the first time, and she shivers.

The apartment is dark except for the purple grow lights in the living room. She stands in Laundry Row. Yes, there is a strange noise. Blurp . . . blurp . . . blurp. It sounds like the bubbles in a fish tank. It seems possible that there is a fish tank in the apartment, buried somewhere under a forgotten mound of something. Blurp . . . blurp. No, the noise is coming from the bathroom, a room she hasn't explored yet. Blurp . . . blurp . . . blurp. She turns on the hallway light and pushes open the bathroom door all the way. No. Her eyes do not see what they see. A black tube sticking out of the water, along with the toes on two feet at the other end of the tub. In between is a person. She flees to the living room and sits down. She throws out her arm, momentarily losing control of herself, and almost knocks over the cage with the large blue and yellow parrot. Large blue and yellow parrot? It's spraying hulls out at her. It was not there earlier, of that she's sure. In fact, none of this was here earlier – she's in the midst of a dream.

Several minutes pass with no answers to simple questions, such as: Was the person who was lying naked with a snorkel really

Random? And, what should she do if it wasn't? And, why was he doing it? But simple questions have simple answers: Random appears in a white terrycloth robe, bare feet, and wet hair. He walks slowly down the hall, and smiles at her, sitting down across the room. "Hi," he says. "I feel wonderful."

"I'm sorry I walked in on you – I had no idea . . . "

"That's okay, really. You can watch any time."

"Thanks." She lets a significant moment elapse. "Just what would I be watching?"

"It's my therapy. My whole group is doing it. We try to get back to conditions in our mother's womb – you know – the most secure time of life."

The light bulb in Miriam's head is not burnt out. It clicks on. So this was the back-to-the-womb therapy. Not lying in a fetal position like any normal person would do to get back to the womb. "No wonder your hands are so wrinkled then!" The instant she says it, she's sorry. His whole body slumps. "I didn't mean anything . . . " she says.

He gets up and mumbles a goodnight, and closes his bedroom door.

Even though she feels guilty for her comment, she decides she's still allowed to use the bathroom. The bathroom in this place is not anywhere you'd want to spend time. As she carefully washes her face, she props her toothbrush on her ear, like a pencil, to avoid putting it on the sink. Only a madman, or someone willing to contract permanent staphylococcus would put a toothbrush on this particular sink. Forget the snorkel hanging on the spigot, forget the bath she has looked forward to in the morning. There is no way in the world her skin will touch that tub. The bathtub ring is corroded into the porcelain like acne scars from a distant adolescence. She manages not to trip on the water bugs wriggling on their backs, and she guesses she'll be able to use the hotel bathroom in the morning.

Sleep does not come easily on the flat leatherette couch which has upholstery buttons every five inches, but she's willing to put up with it as punishment for her remark to Random.

But there is the matter of the immigrant bird. It is sitting right by her head. To entertain herself she leans on her elbows and tries to say something, but he only makes squawking sounds. She loves to see birds flying and building nests, but up close her fondness for birds stopped with Donald Duck. She finally finds the cloth for the cage, and the bird stops squawking, but she can't get to sleep with the scraping and fluttering sounds it makes. She again turns on the light and begins to write Julie a letter:

Dear Julie,

I don't know when your last piece of hate mail arrived, but it has probably been too long, so I thought I'd take up the slack. A gargantuan parrot is perched to my right, popping hulls at me. I won't even talk about the roaches, except every region of the world is represented, and I'll go right on to say, Where's my pillow? And why didn't you tell me to bring your parents' garbage compactor? Beginning to get the picture? The apartment is so awful, that Random spends most of his time in the tub. Yes, I wanted to experience the real New York – not the nightmare New York. Understand? I might come home early. I'm afraid I will stick to something like a chair, and have to spend the rest of my life here. My only wish is that I could throw you in the kitchen, lights off, for ten minutes. Any more time, and not even your bones would be left.

As she finishes, the bedroom door opens. "I saw your light on," Random says. "Sometimes it's hard to sleep in a strange environment. If you'd like to . . . you know . . . hop in with me for the night . . . well that would be all right with me."

Strange environment is right. She smiles at him. "I'm glad you're not mad at me."

He smiles at her, and gestures toward his room. The way he is leaning out the door, half his body is missing. The half she can see is naked.

"My offer is completely kosher," he says. "No strings."

Or pajamas or robes. "I appreciate it," she says. She gets up and tiptoes over to him to ensure as little contact with the rug as possible. She touches him on the arm. "I really haven't tried sleeping yet – if I have any trouble I'll let you know."

He leans around the threshold with a signal that means only

one thing. They kiss softly. "Goodnight," he says, "I sure wish you were staying longer."

*

The next evening she returns to the apartment to collect her suitcases. It is not an unhappy moment of her trip. When she enters the apartment she hears the familiar blurp . . . blurp . . . blurp. She has kept her suitcases tightly locked to prevent anything from crawling inside them. She takes them to the door, and . . . well . . . yes . . . she better say goodbye. She knocks on the bathroom door. Maybe disturbing him will give him some kind of psychological trauma, but in the interests of politeness, she has to chance it. He did say she could watch.

He doesn't respond. The snorkel tube, sticking up like a piece of electrified licorice, doesn't move either. She tiptoes to the tub and stands over it. The body looks too white – like it's a piece of clay that hasn't been fired. Maybe he's dead. What would she possibly tell the police with an unclothed body sporting a snorkel? They would think some form of sexual perversion at least. But just then Random opens his eyes. The Lock Ness monster emerges from Davy Jones's locker:

"Hi," he says.

"Hi."

"I'm just going under. The longer you stay, the farther back you go."

"Farther back?"

"Yeah, to your origins. Some people are able to get to the fish – to really feel like a fish – to feel their fish heritage."

She involuntarily touches the side of her neck. Does he breathe through gills? "I'm leaving, Random," she says, her voice rising as if it were struck by deep emotion.

"So soon? You just got here." He smiles at her. "Were things laid back at the convention?"

Somehow she can't think of her talks with history professors as laid back. "Well . . . uh . . . " she says, deftly avoiding the question, "I guess I'll go now."

"Give Julie my love, and tell her to come visit soon. I've got some crazies I want her to meet. Tell her I'm doing a lot better. She'll know what I mean." Then he gives her directions for going to the airport on public transportation, even though they both know she's going to catch a cab. He squirms out of the snorkel, and reaches up for her, and they kiss. Yes, she gets wet, but if she says anything, like, do you have to drip so much all over my clean clothes, she might offend him. Neither of them thinks it strange that he is kissing her goodby naked, with a mascot snorkel. It's how things are in this apartment: squalor and snorkels and skin.

Outside the apartment door she leaves a paper sack containing an African violet. Some heritage within her probably going back further than fish, has caused her to buy a thank you gift. That it should have been a Venus fly trap just occurs to her.

Taking a plane was a last minute indulgence because people in her family always took the train from Chicago to New York and back. On the flight home she rereads the letter she wrote to Julie, and is glad she didn't send it. Sending it would have been an easy way out for her cousin. No, she will urge her to visit, instead; implore her to visit, telling her that Random needs her, that he's having trouble – that he's going under more and more, and only she can help, an old friend, a shoulder to cry on. And of course she will be sure not to mention anything about the apartment. Two breadcrumbs out of place can send Julie up the wall. She won't go overboard and say it's so clean you can eat off the floor. Julie would never believe that because the only floor in the world clean enough to eat off of was their Aunt Rose's, and Aunt Rose is safely tucked underground with a carpet of grass above. Bleach was Aunt Rose's secret weapon. That kind of clean doesn't exist anymore. But if she doesn't mention anything, that will be implying that things are all right. And when Julie says something, as she certainly will when she comes back from her visit to Random, Miriam will respond with, "Really? That bad? It wasn't like that when I was there." On the other hand, she can't help seeing Random's doughy white body floating in the tub, and she leans back, trying to concentrate on her insidious plot, but something won't let her. God and her body know how much she wants to relax, but that white form, hovering in the tub like a beached whale, won't quite let her enjoy her scheme.

Henry Africa's

DORY AND I walk into Henry Africa's and it's crowded and people at the bar are singing and I say, we're just going to have one drink because you know what happens when I have more.

We sit down at a long wooden table and I look over at Dory; her nipples are arching against her sweater, and she's got her legs crossed high, and she suddenly says, let's move over there quick. Before I realize it, we're sitting in two lounge chairs with a little marble table in between, and the waitress has just taken our order for Irish coffee. I curl up in the chair and I'm about to say something to Dory, something stupid, like isn't this an interesting place, or I wonder what kind of plant that is – there are hundreds of plants all around – but I can't because she's watching several men at a table about two feet away and I could light a match by her eyes and she wouldn't move she's so involved in looking at them, and I chuckle and want to say, why don't you be a little obvious or something. I start playing the game of I wonder which one she wants. She'll tell me for sure in a few minutes when she'll just happen to suggest we go to the bathroom, and she'll talk about the odds of this one as opposed to that one, and which one do I think would go in for the weird stuff, because, she'll say, you know I don't want any of that, just a good lay to make me think this trip to San Francisco has been worth it.

Why she thinks of me as an expert on who'll be good for a night in bed, I don't know. But she's always asking my opinion of what I think a man will be like. Well, I usually say, you know I've been seeing Art for three years so it's kind of hard for me to evaluate things. And she usually responds with, yeah, but before that . . . and I say, but that was a long time ago, and Art and I have it good. If it hadn't been for his New York business trip, he would have probably come here with me.

I'm sipping my Irish coffee through the whipped cream, getting a sinking feeling because it only costs fifty cents, and at that price I know I'm going to drink more than one, which means I'll get drunk and Dory isn't exactly a person to depend on.

She leans towards me and points to a man in a paisley shirt, who glances at her, working his eyes over her slowly. He's eye-fucking you, I want to say, but I don't. Well, what do you think of him, she says. Weird, he definitely goes in for weird stuff, I tell her, hardly able to keep from smirking. You think so, she asks seriously. I shrug. So she doesn't believe me. Well, I really had no idea when I told her. I just said it to say something.

She raises her skirt a little higher, and the waitress comes over and gives her another drink and says that a man at the next table would like her to join him. She smiles and says to me, do you mind, and I say no, but I'll just sit here. I watch her ass wiggle away, and I'm really happy I only wore blue jeans and a shirt instead of the Indian print dress with the low front that she almost talked me into wearing. This is her night. She had let me know that she thought her decision to stay with me at my aunt's house was a huge mistake; I'll even have to fabricate some excuse for her if I go home alone because Aunt Sylvia, always curious, will be shocked if I tell her the truth.

All of a sudden she's standing up and signaling me to follow her, and I do, reluctantly, because I'm comfortable and getting high, and we walk the length of the room and up some steps to the washroom and I watch as men stare at her as we walk. When we get inside, she says, well, what do you think of him. I already told you, I say, you know, I said he was into weird stuff. Oh, Natalie, not that one, she says; no, the other one, the one with the checked shirt – he's the one. What do you think of him. I think to myself, you're a pretty fast operator, and I smile and say aloud that I once made it with a man who wore a checked shirt and he was pretty good, pretty damn good, and she purses her lips and gives me a slight push on the shoulder and says, oh go to hell, now tell me really, what do you think. She's frowning at me, angry that I'm teasing her. I know she wants me to tell her he's okay; she's already made her decision and she just wants a seal of approval so to speak, a kind of guarantee that he'll be good or she'll get some kind of refund. Well, if it's the one I think it is, he's good looking, I say tentatively, watching to see if that will do. She smiles. It was the right thing to say. You think so . . . I think he is too. She fluffs up the curls on her head and squirts on some more perfume, and says, let's go.

We go out and down the steps, and she says, oh, since you'll probably be going home first, and your aunt will still be awake, let me take the key. I search around for the key in my pocket. It's got a little plastic poodle attached, a constant reminder of Aunt Sylvia. She takes it and swings it around a minute and then says, you're not mad, are you. Nope, I say; you have fun, but be careful and phone for god's-sake if things get rough.

She prances off, and I go back to my drink, and she talks to the man in the checked shirt. He stands, and he's tall and for one wild second he reminds me of Art, and I wonder what Art is doing at this very minute. He could be sitting in a hotel bar somewhere in New York, and maybe, if he meets a woman . . . I finish the rest of my drink and order another and a man with red hair who's about five-nine comes over and sits down at my table, and he's paying the waitress for his drink, and when I take out money for mine, he says, oh, I just paid for it. I notice that Dory is walking toward the exit, and she turns for an instant and waves. The man at my table smiles at me; he's looking at me with a look that I haven't seen in quite a while – a look that says I'm interested in you, woman, and how about it. I smile back, wanting to buy time because I didn't count on this. I have to evaluate the situation, but I'm lousy in a panic. He's talking, telling me about some trivial incident that's happened across the room, and he's reaching over and touching my fingers as he's talking, watching my reaction to that, and I start drinking faster than usual, and then remember that's the worst thing I could do because I should keep clear headed, but before I know it, there's another Irish coffee in its place, and he's asking me my name. I tell him; he says it's pretty, and even though I think he says it just to make pleasant conversation, I can't help being a little flattered. What's yours, I say. Carl. We smile at each other, and I take another sip of my drink.

I feel uncomfortable for a moment, like something's expected of me and I can't deliver. Carl is telling me what a nice night it is out there. Well, I've still got this whole drink, I point out, and then say, what do you do for a living, just to keep talking. I usually hate that question when it's asked so directly – like an interview. He looks down at his glass, and twists it around for a minute and looks up and laughs, a little embarrassed. You won't believe it, he says. No, what, I ask, curious. Well, he says, I play cards for money.

It's the last thing I expect him to come up with. I think of Art and his job as company lawyer, and they're probably around the same age – thirty – and I wonder what Art would think about his woman going out with a card shark.

Well, Carl says, at least if you won't check out the great night with me, you'll let me drive you home. He's got me. What could the harm be in that, I think. He's already mentioned he lives near Golden Gate Park, and that's the area where I'm staying, so I say okay, and he smiles, and I get a slight uneasy feeling that somehow I've said okay to more than just a drive home, but I don't quite know how I've done it.

We walk out, and his arm is around me, and we go down Geary Street and around the corner where his jeep is parked. He opens the door for me, which Art stopped doing about a week after I met him, and before I get in he kisses me first on the forehead, and then, slowly, on the lips, and when I don't back away, he kisses harder and I touch his side and run my hand around his back, and I think, decisions aren't so difficult after all.

He tells me that he wants to stop by his apartment for a second to walk the dog, she'll be going crazy, is that okay. All right, I say, fidgeting a little; that sounds contrived, and I wonder if he does live near Golden Gate Park; maybe he's a maniac or something, and I'll never make it to the airport tomorrow. If I could give Art a call, this would all be over. But then I figure, I've already made the choice, and if he's going to murder me or something, he's going to do it – I'm in his clutches – but chances are he's not going to, so maybe I should just see what happens and relax.

The neighborhood does look familiar, and we park in front of a white stucco building with arches, and he says, this is it. We get out and walk in the door and he takes my hand as we walk up a flight of stairs. A dog is barking and Carl opens the door, and a large white Labrador jumps on him. We walk in, and he snaps on the light and he says, hey, let me walk her for a second, and I'll be back and we'll have a drink.

I wait, thumbing through a magazine, trying to read it, but I can't, and I hear the dog barking outside from a distance. I look around; there's a whole wall of books and that surprises me. I start looking at them and I notice how he has them arranged in fiction, non-fiction and poetry like we do in the bookstore I work at back in Chicago.

Finally Carl returns. He's left the dog in the hallway, which he tells me is where she likes to sleep. I follow him into the kitchen which has dishes scattered on counters, and he begins to make tea. He pushes dishes aside to make room for two cups, and we stand there waiting for the water to boil.

We walk back into the living room with our tea, which is steaming and hard to drink. We sit on the floor and put the cups down. They're like little geysers puffing away. Carl puts his hands on my shoulders and looks at me, and then we kiss, my teeth pressing against his, and his muscles are taut, and he pulls my shirt out from my jeans and touches my skin underneath and I all of a sudden hug him, having no idea how much I wanted to hug someone, and how long it's been since I really have.

He unbuttons the rest of my shirt, and we kiss again, and he tugs me along to the bedroom. We lie down on the bed, which has a jumble of covers all over and we push them aside. It's very dark in the room and I can only see a vague outline of him. I hear him unzipping, and kicking off his shoes, and I start doing the same, slowly though, remembering how when Art and I first made love he carefully undressed me which made me feel like a doll or something; Carl reaches over and feels that I've still got on my jeans so he waits a second while I peel them off. Our bodies touch and we hold each other, rolling around, and then we kiss, lips, neck, and he softly between my legs and I between his, and we continue touching.

We make love for the rest of the night, whatever's left of it, sleeping on and off, waking, our bodies still sweaty against one another, and finally by morning his face emerges in the light, and I begin to notice that he's got freckles all over him, but especially on his back and I start to count them and he says five thousand and we laugh.

We lie embracing, and he says, I could stay like this all day, couldn't you, and I say, yes, I wish I could, but I have to catch my plane back to Chicago at noon.

We rise slowly from the damp sheets, wandering around naked, gathering up pieces of clothing, and we head for the bathroom. I hate to wake up in the morning, I tell him, as he turns on the shower. Yeah, he says, who likes to.

He makes us some tea, and this time we drink it, sitting at his kitchen table, and I begin to think about getting back to Chicago, and it kind of feels like a relief to know that. Then I remember I'll be seeing Art tonight – a big reunion probably after our week's separation – lobster at Nantucket Cove where we've gone for holidays and birthdays – and a lazy romantic time back at his apartment – candles burning, and if I give it some thought for a minute or two, I will probably be able to name the records in the order that he'll put them on the stereo.

Well, Natalie, let's go. Carl stands and kisses me on the head and pulls me up and we hug for a moment and walk out into the hall where his dog, Bonita, is growling at the downstairs door. He snaps on her leash and we walk down the street, stopping for a moment as she pees, and then walking back to his jeep where the three of us get in.

I tell him the address which it turns out is about five blocks away. Hey, he says, it's only nine o'clock; how about walking along the beach for a little while. Bonita is whining in the back. I say, I wish I could, but I have a lot to do, and I think to myself that probably Aunt Sylvia has called the police by now and there's a dragnet around the city. Besides the night is over, and I kind of want to get away, get more in the mood for Chicago, but I don't tell him that. Well, he says, I sure wish you would change your mind; it's really beautiful this time of day.

We pull up in front of my aunt's house and I lean over and we kiss, and I step down from the jeep and linger at the door for a moment and then close it and he drives off. And I feel god-damned empty as I watch the jeep disappear around a corner two blocks away.

I walk up the stone steps which are lined with clay flowerpots on each side, and I ring the bell reluctantly, and angry that I gave up my key to Dory, whom I remember for the first time since last night.

Aunt Sylvia answers, in her terrycloth robe. She frowns at me and doesn't say anything, and I think that maybe I should have phoned her to tell her I wouldn't be home. Her angry stare makes me feel like I'm under a floodlight. I know she feels responsible for me while I'm visiting her, and there's no way to tell her not to worry.

Dory runs down the stairs in her bathrobe and says, Jesus, Natalie, we nearly went insane wondering where the hell you were. She's peering at me closely, trying to determine what has occurred, trying to see if the words *I got laid* are somehow written on me like a sign. I stand in front of a gigantic fern which is on a Greek-styled pedestal, and my aunt finally says, well, at least you're alive, and I don't say anything because all the harm she can do is to call the Chicago branch of the family and tell them what a wild disreputable life I lead.

Dory's standing on the stairs, bobbing back and forth, so I say I'm going to pack, and we go up and I ask her first what happened to her. She wrinkles up her nose at me and says, nothing much happened, nothing at all. I squint at her and say, huh, and she tells me that the man she left with practically tore her clothes off in the car. She managed to get away, and she caught a taxi back to my aunt's. I then tell her what happened to me, and she looks at me enviously and says, how many times did you do it, and I say, I lost count, and laugh as she walks to the bathroom in a huff, and I hear her slamming down something on the counter.

As I start gathering my clothes together, slowly, I hear the phone ringing in the distance. There's about a minute pause between when it stops and when my aunt's voice calls my name. I let a skirt droop into the suitcase and open the door, and she says, Natalie, again, loud, and I say, yeah, and she says, Art's on the phone calling from Chicago. I'll get it in your room, I say, and walk across the hall and pick up the receiver and say, okay, and wait for the click which tells me she's hung up downstairs.

He talks to me excitedly: hi babe, how was your trip, but his words start merging together, and I answer in yeses and nos and sures and all rights and I find myself drawing designs on a notepad my aunt has on the nightstand, and I see Carl running along the beach with Bonita. The more Art talks, the more I'm overwhelmed with a heavy thick feeling inside, and I sink into the mattress where I'm sitting, and I think, god, at least I should have gone and walked on the beach for a little while; why the hell didn't I do that; it would have probably been nice. Art's voice comes back into focus, and he says, honey, are you listening, and I say, I could have gone walking along the ocean this morning with a friend and I didn't, and he says, what, and I say, oh nothing, go on with what you were telling me, and he does. I keep smelling the heavy smell in the room when Carl and I woke this morning, and remembering how he rubbed soap over me in the shower, and why the hell didn't I go to the beach for a few minutes. I put the receiver down on the pillow and hear Art's angry excited voice get muffled, and then he clicks the button on his end several times, and it finally stops – all that noise – and I hang up, knowing that when I get back to Chicago I can explain things, fix things up, if I want to.

Uncertain Geographies

I AM DRIVING in Chicago. I get a red light at Clark and North near the $1 Village Theater. It's my first red light ever in the city because I've never driven here before. I drive on, past the strand of Lincoln Park that borders Clark Street, past the laundry that I always peek into to see if the men are still running it from when I lived here fifteen years ago. On previous visits when I rode by on a city bus, the man with the strawberry blond wisps on his bald head was behind the counter making change and taking in the dry cleaning. His partner was behind him putting a dress on the form and inflating the wrinkles out with a white fog of steam. It made me feel good to see them, as if I could move right into my apartment again, and bring my laundry there the next weekend in the pillowcases with the bright tulips stamped on them. My head does a left turn toward the window of the laundry, and there's a clerk, but he's not the same one. He's taller and younger. I know every twist of Clark Street, I've been into almost every store that I pass, I could walk blindfolded to the specials bin at Bargains Unlimited further up on my left, and yet no one would recognize me anymore if I walked into one of these places.

I turn west, coming up on the intersection of Lincoln, Halsted, and Fullerton. When I lived in Chicago years ago, I didn't know how to drive. I always thought this wacky, slanted intersection would be impossible to drive through. But the lights for the cars seem sensibly placed, and I breeze across before I realize that I've accomplished what I once assumed was something I could never do. The Seminary Restaurant is on the west corner. This time its neon *Y* is on the fritz, and the early bird customers are being welcomed to the Seminar Restaurant. I've never had the privilege of seeing sunlight through the plate glass window, but I know the depths of the Seminary, in the darkest parts of the night, two or three A.M. when I went for a very early breakfast, sitting in a booth with cotton batting blooming through rips in the vinyl upholstery.

I get to my destination: my mother's basement apartment on Olive Street. Olive is one way going the wrong way, so I circle around the block in order to park. I am clearing out her apartment, deciding what she can take to Florida, and what she can't. She is in the hospital, four miles further north, waiting for me to pick through her things. Sometimes I drive to the hospital, but mostly I'm at the apartment. She has given me orders I can't obey – to save things that can't be shipped. Huge air conditioners that breathe for her worn-out lungs in the summer; a freezer that stores mountains of food so she doesn't have to shop often.

"Rachel, I need those things," she tells me on the phone.

"They have them in Florida too," I assure her.

"But they're paid for," she says. "I just finished paying off the freezer on my Sears charge last month. . . ."

My mother's Sears charge has been her reentry into the world. She can no longer take the Clark bus to the Loop to shop at the real Sears. She can no longer walk two blocks to the grocery store. She has her personal Sears lady. In the past I've heard her telephoning, asking for Arlene. She ordered some pale blue sheets for me, two shirts for my husband, short-sleeved polyester, and brown corduroy house slippers for him too. Now in the hospital there is no more Sears lady. I explain to my mother on the phone that U.P.S. does not ship air conditioners and freezers. I hear her sigh. Besides, I think, my Florida house can't hold other people's things that are the size or weight of baby whales.

I have a cousin in Chicago named Freddy. The most I can say

about him is he's a big bear of a someone who has a memorable hug. He grew up in Philadelphia while I was doing the same in Chicago. Now he works in Chicago. I try to call him Fred when I talk to him, but I'm so used to hearing my mother refer to him as Freddy that the child name slips out. He doesn't seem to mind. Freddy is going to drive my mother and me to the airport when we leave at the end of the week. He will stay with us until we are on the plane.

My mother has told me that when she was pregnant six months, she had to take Freddy in. His mother became ill after his birth, and my mother offered to keep him. She raised him that first year until his mother became stronger. Then he was returned and never told what happened. "I was carrying your brother, inside," my mother always says, "and had Freddy propped on my hip. I must have been a sight."

*

I have vowed never to come to Chicago again in January, but that's when my mother always gets struck. Her emphysema is clogging her lungs and gets worse in cold weather. I get off the plane from Florida. It is twenty-eight below zero. I am prepared with a fisherman's sweater, a wool hat and lengthy muffler, and two pairs of mittens worn piggy-back. Everything is borrowed from friends in Florida, taken out of storage for this occasion. No one ever wears things like this down there, but everyone has some fossil of a life up North waiting to be excavated from mothballs. My contribution is a yellow ski jacket, a thin epidermis for its bulky sweater interior.

I get to my friend Nell's apartment in the afternoon. As I walk from the limo bus, I realize that it's probably the coldest weather I've ever walked in.

I go to visit my mother at the hospital after I drop my things at Nell's. There is a red sign on the door that says: "Oxygen in Use – No Smoking." I have not seen my mother in a year, and she has warned me in our many phone calls that she has changed, lost weight, I won't recognize her. I find her sunken into her bed. She lets out a cry when she spots me at the door. I bend down and hug her, weaving my arms through the oxygen tubes. Her skin is hot, like sidewalks in summer. I wonder if I would have recognized her if I hadn't known she was in this room. But how can you not know your mother, and after only a year?

"This is Dee-Dee, my daughter," she says, turning her head to her roommate, another woman sunken into a bed. My mother tells me the woman's name. Something beginning with *M*. I won't remember it. I have met so many of these women in beds next to my mother's that their names blur in my mind.

"Dee-Dee is thirty-six, can you believe it?" my mother tells her roommate. The woman smiles. My mother calls me by a name that is not mine. She always wanted to name me Deirdre so she could call me Dee-Dee. Instead I was named Rachel. But now she calls me Dee-Dee. She has never called me by this foreign name before, but maybe she has been thinking this name to herself my whole life.

"Thirty-six," my mother repeats. "I can't believe it."

I twist a dead blossom off a flower arrangement by her bed. I suppose my age seems young to my mother at seventy-five. She tells me her roommate is going home later in the day. These women in the next bed named Margaret or Madge or Pearl have left her in the hospital for years. They are always going home before her.

"Dee-Dee, don't forget my robe," she says as I'm leaving.

There is that name again. My mother has thought of me as an entirely different person for as long as I have been alive.

*

Every morning it's the same. I leave Nell's apartment building through a door held open by a man in uniform, and walk across the street to a similar building. I ask for Nell's car in the garage and it is brought to me. I always tip the car hop even though Nell says I don't have to.

I learned to drive after I moved to Florida. I always assumed driving here would be a mystery I would never solve. Right away I'm on a narrow street that is supposed to be two way. As I drive, everything is obscured by the heavy white exhaust fumes that become visible in the frostbitten temperatures. I go slowly and I'm terrified. The air itself is frozen and I have to crack through it to make progress. I am driving in Chicago, ghosts weaving around the car. As I drive along, I relax some. Everyone else is driving slowly too. Questions begin to occur to me, like what is the speed limit and can you turn right on red? I know where to go, what street to turn at, that Lake Michigan is to my right, hovering over my shoulder half a mile away, a lake that changes colors with the seasons and ups its temperature in late July so people can swim in it for exactly a month. I know everything about this place even though I've been away a long time. I still use a street map for navigation in the Florida city I've lived in for years. If we drive out of our neighborhood, my husband Sam sometimes quizzes me: "Which way is east?" I stare at him for a moment. I might as well point up or down. "East is away from the Gulf," he tells me. "Don't you know?" I tell him that east is not away from the Gulf. It's in another time zone, the direction *toward* water. My geography is inside me. It has nothing to do with landscape anymore. I never had to use a street map in Chicago.

*

Every night it's the same. I drive the car back to the garage and go across to Nell's building. We hug each other in greeting. Parts of our lives are lost to each other because we live over a thousand miles apart. I bring back another bottle of expensive wine that I've found in strange places in my mother's apartment: among the scarves in her dresser and in the silverware drawer. "Wine bottles break in shipping," I reason, as we open a bottle and usually finish it.

The apartment is cleared now. Once I packed up the things to ship, I felt nothing for the other knickknacks and furniture I sold to a dealer. I bring the car back to Nell's. With an entire afternoon to kill, I take the bus downtown, have lunch at Carson's, get my hair styled at a salon, and walk over to the Art Institute. Now it's warmer and the sun is shining. I'm still dressed in my crazy clothes, minus the leg warmers under my corduroys, minus one pair of mittens. I walk up the steps of the Art Institute and push through the revolving door. I love revolving doors and there don't seem to be any where I live in Florida. I spend the afternoon roaming the galleries, visiting paintings that I have particularly missed: Rembrandt's *Young Woman at a Half-Open Door*, Seurat's *An Afternoon on La Grand Jatte*, Picasso's *Blue Guitarist*. I am an intruder here. I no longer flash a membership card. I pay an admission price.

*

We are at the airport. My mother, in a wheelchair, is wearing a bright striped velour top that I gave her for a birthday. The shirt is gallon-sized on her demitasse body. Her face is difficult to locate behind her glasses. She is chattering to Freddy who is pushing her chair. We board the airplane, Freddy still pushing. I go first and sit near a window. Oxygen canisters are in place in the middle seat. My mother reaches up and hugs Freddy, her eyes riveted onto his when the hug has eased. She is seeing him as a tiny child when she cared for him, as all mothers see their children at times. I do not know if he has heard the story of his beginning months. But there is no longer time to tell him.

We taxi onto the runway. A light snow is drifting down. It is the last glimpse of snow my mother will ever have. "We got on just in time," she says.

*

One block in Chicago is an eighth of a mile. In South Shore or Rogers Park a block is the same. Joggers can tell exactly how far they've run. There's something comforting in knowing what distance you've covered or how far it is to someplace. On a visit a few years ago, I was staying at Nell's also. I'd leave her building and jog around the block, past Hugh Hefner's mansion with the sawhorses at the curb to hold parking spaces, all the way around past the Ambassador West Hotel. Twice around meant I had gone a mile. I am taking my mother to a city in Florida where you have to drive a car along a jogging route to figure out the mileage on the odometer. Every block is a different length. The lovely pink sidewalks, iridescent with chunks of quartz, do not make up for this haphazardness. Chicago sidewalks are plain, with the date they were poured stamped into them. They know how long they are, and where they came from.

During the eleven years she lived in Florida, Karen Loeb always considered herself a midwesterner-at-large. Her roots are in the Midwest, specifically Chicago, and a number of the stories in the book grow from that location.

Loeb has published stories, poems, and articles in many magazines and newspapers including *The North American Review,* the *South Dakota Review, The St. Petersburg Times* and *The Orlando Sentinel.* Two of her stories have won PEN Syndicated Fiction awards, and she has received literary grants from the Florida Arts Council and the Wisconsin Arts Board, including a fellowship and grant from Wisconsin in 1990 and 1991.

After teaching in St. Petersburg, Florida, she returned to the Midwest in order to teach creative writing and other courses at the University of Wisconsin-Eau Claire. She has an M.F.A. in fiction writing from Bowling Green State University. Currently she's at work on a book of related stories that span a sixty-year period and focus on family relationships in Chicago.

About the Cover
Karen Tucker Kuykendall is an award-winning artist from Tampa, Florida, whose paintings have been exhibited throughout the southeastern United States. The cover art, done especially for this book, is a 15″ x 15″ oil on paper.